D0306953

OGILVIE AND THE GOLD OF THE RAJ

Philip McCutchan

Severn House Large Print
London & New York

This first large print edition published in Great Britain 2005 by
SEVERN HOUSE LARGE PRINT BOOKS LTD of
9-15 High Street, Sutton, Surrey, SM1 1DF.
First world regular print edition published 2003 by
Severn House Publishers, London and New York.
This first large print edition published in the USA 2005 by
SEVERN HOUSE PUBLISHERS INC., of
595 Madison Avenue, New York, NY 10022.

British Library Cataloguing in Publication Data

McCutchan, Philip, 1920 -
Ogilvie and the gold of the Raj. - Large print ed.
1. Great Britain. Army - Fiction
2. Ogilvie, James (Fictitious character) - Fiction
3. India - History - 19th century - Fiction
4. Historical fiction
5. Large type books
I. Title II. MacNeil, Duncan, 1920 -. Train at Bundarbar
823.9'14 [F]

ISBN 0-7278-7416-0

Printed and bound in Great Britain by
MPG Books Ltd, Bodmin, Cornwall.

One

It had rained without cease for days past – days that had run into a matter of weeks by the time the First Division with its headquarters staff and its massive transport columns had been ordered to move east for Bengal from Nowshera and Peshawar. While the Supply and Transport with their horses, mules, camels and assorted wagons and carts moved slowly by their own efforts, the infantry battalions moved faster and a little more comfortably by the train. A little more comfortably but not much; the troop trains were vastly over-crowded and the facilities were few. Only in the splendid coach occupied by Lieutenant-General Francis Fettleworth and his senior staff officers – a coach reminiscent of Her Majesty's own drawing-room coach plying to and from Balmoral in far-off Scotland – was there any real comfort. Here Bloody Francis, as the Divisional Commander was known to his subordinates, sprawled inelegantly in a brocaded armchair blaspheming at the *punkah-wallahs* and demanding *chota pegs* from his swaying pantry. In the regimental officers' coaches conditions were far less tolerable, but as compared with those suffered by the rank and file they were comfortable enough. The privates and junior NCOs were packed like sardines, sweating swatting at the abounding flies, avid for the halts when food and toilet facilities of a sort awaited them. As they left the lands of the North-West Frontier and began to come into the teeming rain, it all became worse. There was a horrible fug, and khaki-drill uniforms became limp and damp and the kilts of the Royal Strathspey clung clammily to knees and thighs.

Major Lord Brora, second-in-command of the Scots battalion, stared frowning from the window of his coach at the appalling prospect: already the floods could be seen, not yet deep but beginning to approach the railway track. If ordered to proceed beyond Patna, the division would have to leave the train as the flood-waters closed over the line ahead. Brora swore bad-temperedly; the Colonel glanced at him with distaste, and Brora caught the look.

'I dislike *swimming* in uniform,' he said in an acid voice. 'I much doubt if Calcutta will have organised half enough boats to carry a division. Colonel!'

'Then we shall wait at Patna until they have!'

'We shall be upon our bottoms for a damn month! No doubt we shall find ourselves pressed into service to bale the damn paddy fields and save the rice—'

'If we are so ordered,' Dornoch interrupted evenly.

'Well, Colonel, it's far from my idea of soldiering. Flood relief my backside! There will be pestilence, what's more. Better to let the buggers drown and take their damn diseases with them for the good of the country.'

Lord Dornoch once again stared at his fellow peer with ill-concealed dislike. 'Indian service is not all fighting, Major. Part of our job is to help the natives and give succour when needed – and now there is a need, with millions likely to find themselves homeless. When you've been longer in India, perhaps you'll understand.'

Brora gave a snort. He said, 'Well while Division's doing its succouring, the damn Pathans are likely to take their chance. Fettleworth's denuded all the blasted garrisons ... for my money. Colonel, there'll be fighting soon enough, with the Frontier so well ablaze that all the damn flood-waters in Bengal won't put it out!'

Brora's point was a valid one and Dornoch knew it. It had been considered by Sir Iain Ogilvie at Northern Army headquarters in

Murree, and by Fettleworth at Division in Nowshera; but the orders from the Viceroy in Calcutta had been precise and urgent. Every available man was needed in Bengal to save life, and the garrisons of Northern Army were to be left with little more than the barrack guards, plus the artillery who would not be required to move out and some cavalry detachments from the native Indian Army units, such as Skinner's Horse and the Guides, who would be left to maintain skeleton patrols. The rest, under the overall command of Lieutenant-General Fettleworth, were to move east at short notice; Sir Iain himself was to remain in Murree and guard the Frontier as best he could with his depleted army corps. Full despatches had arrived from Calcutta: the Ganges, the glacier-fed river that merged with the Brahmaputra to discharge into the immense delta of the Sundarbans between the Hooghli and the Meghna Rivers, was in colossal flood. An eight-foot high wave was sweeping down the river, muddy and vicious and tremendously fast, and was expected to engulf Patna within the next few days. The deaths would be many, the devastation of the land calamitous; Lord Elgin, Viceroy of India, intended deploying the full strength of the Raj to alleviate distress. Already medical teams had moved in upon the areas from which the flood-waters had receded in their passage east, and from Patna to Calcutta itself more doctors were standing by with disinfectants and medicines to combat the anticipated outbreaks of cholera and malaria.

Within hours of the orders being received, the 114th Highlanders, the Queen's Own Royal Strathspey, with their brigaded battalions from the Peshawar cantonment, had been marched to the railway station and the troop trains. It was to be a new experience and a humane one; but, even though the march was not to war, Mr Cunningham, Regimental Sergeant-Major, and the colour-sergeants had been as eagle-eyed as ever for smartness and precision as the battalion moved off by companies to the sound of the pipes and drums.

Under their section sergeants the men piled out onto the platform at Patna railway station, bare and wet with rain that sliced down like a battery of knives, rain so hard that it bounced up from the ground as it landed, soaking spats and kilts as it were from below. James Ogilvie, marching along the platform to oversee the detraining of B Company, was hailed by the Adjutant, Andrew Black.

'Captain Ogilvie!'

Ogilvie halted. Black came up like a bony vulture, sour and sardonic and already wet to the skin; even his moustache, as black as his name, drooped with the rain.

Black said, 'A plague on the weather! You know the orders, do you not, Ogilvie?'

'Yes.'

'Then kindly repeat them to me.'

Ogilvie stared. 'Now look—'

'Do as I say, if you please, without argument. I wish to be sure that all company commanders know the orders precisely.'

'Very well, Captain Black,' Ogilvie said formally. 'The battalion is to march to the Roman Catholic cathedral where the men will be billeted overnight. All officers of the division will be accommodated in the government college. Picquets are to be posted—'

'As though we were in the field, yes. Full alertness, Captain Ogilvie. There may be looting, and this must be put down firmly. Likewise riot. The natives are in the habit of blaming the British for any misfortunes, and we may face trouble.' Black paused, and pulled at his moustache as though in an attempt to wring the wet from it. 'And the orders in that connection, Captain Ogilvie?'

'Firm but tactful handling. No avoidable bloodshed, no provocation—'

'Exactly. You have it. Questions will be asked in Calcutta if there should be any deviation from this. Company commanders will be held responsible.' Again the Adjutant paused. 'Further orders are expected in the morning, when General Fettleworth has reviewed the situation. Carry on, if you please, Captain Ogilvie.'

Black swung away to make himself a nuisance to the other company commanders. Ogilvie moved on towards B Company. Black was an old woman; the orders had been concisely passed down by Fettleworth's Chief of Staff and only a fool could have failed to take them in, but Black, as well as being an old woman, was one who liked always to say things twice so that he couldn't be accused later of any sins of omission. And, of course, it was true that circumspection was going to be called for in the handling of the native population, ever suspicious of British motives and likely enough to be more than usually so when descended upon by so vast a military expedition as an entire infantry division, which could be a provocation in itself. Meanwhile, the orders in that respect held danger for the company commanders and the NCOs, dangers that Colour-Sergeant MacTrease commented on as the Scots fell in for the march to the cathedral.

'If there's trouble, sir, it may be difficult to hold the men.'

'But not impossible, Colour.'

'No, sir. Only I have it in mind they're going to resent trouble – say, stoning, sir –

when they're here to help.'

Ogilvie nodded. 'I realise that, Colour, but the orders are very clear. You'll have to impress on the Jocks that this is a time for turning the other cheek.'

'Aye, sir,' MacTrease answered, sounding dour about it. The military always got the dirty end of the stick and afterwards they got the blame as well. Listening to some sour comment from the ranks as the men moved off, MacTrease felt as though he were sitting on a bomb. As the battalion began its march, slopping through as yet shallow flood-water into the rain-swept city, Lord Brora, his horse now brought from the horse-van, rode down the files of Scots brandishing a riding-crop. He rode a little ahead of the advance, stood in his stirrups, and gave loud tongue.

'Remember you're to be billeted in a cathedral. Holy ground ... so no damn swearing or blasphemy or Division'll have the blasted clergy round its ears like a swarm of damn black beetles. If that happens, the General will have every man's balls for breakfast.'

Brora turned his horse and rode up behind the Colonel as the pipes and drums beat out into the downpour.

It was a highly curious sight as Cunningham and the Regimental Quarter-Master Sergeant bedded the men down, by sections, into their pews for the night. The pulpit loomed, as did sundry religious effigies, and there was an overall smell of incense to fight a battle against the smell of wet cloth. A priest, an Englishman, had bid them a welcome as the ranks had broken and the men had filed in. When Ogilvie had uttered a smiling apology for the military intrusion, Father Porter had smiled back and said, 'It's not a military occasion, is it? You come not as Cromwell came ... you come to help the needy. We'll do all we can to make your men comfortable.'

Ogilvie thanked him, then turned as the RSM marched up with his helmet beneath his left arm and slammed to the halt. 'Well, Mr Cunningham, you have a baffled look. What's the trouble?'

'No trouble, Captain Ogilvie, no trouble at all. It's going to be easy enough. I'll not be needing to line up the pews as I would the shelter-tents, sir! They're lined up already. If I look baffled as you say, then it's because this is no place for shouting orders.' Cunningham grinned. 'That comes hard on any sar'nt-major, sir!'

Ogilvie gave a chuckle. 'If you want to command attention, use the pulpit – right, Father Porter?'

'It might be a way of sending them all to sleep,' the priest said, somewhat forlornly.

Cunningham smiled. 'I'll be bearing it in mind, sir.' He paused. 'I was meaning to ask about the picquets, Captain Ogilvie. The battalion has the duty for the night, and B Company's on the roster for the first watch. Will I get Colour-Sar'nt MacTrease to detail cathedral and college guards, sir?'

'If you please, Sar'nt-Major.'

Cunningham turned away and marched back along the aisle. Some fifteen minutes later Ogilvie detached from the cathedral with his subalterns, leaving the RSM to watch over the provision of supper for the Scots – a frugal meal of broth prepared by the field kitchens mounted outside the cathedral and protected by canvas screening from the rain. That rain lashed down on Ogilvie as he and his company officers, and, marching separately, the college picquet as detailed, made their way to the government college. Here there was a degree of comfort; a lecture room had been turned into a makeshift mess for the regimental officers, with another apartment set aside for the staff. A bar had been set up, and Ogilvie had ordered a *chota peg* each for himself and his subalterns when Brigadier-General Lakenham, Fettleworth's Chief of Staff, entered and approached Lord Dornoch, the senior infantry colonel of the First Division. There was a brief conversation, then Dornoch called for the officers to give their attention to the Chief of Staff.

'Thank you, gentlemen,' Lakenham said as the conversation fell away. 'I'll not keep you long – and nor, I fancy, will events.' He cleared his throat. 'The civil authorities here in Patna have not been slow to confer with General Fettleworth. There are reports that the rise of the Ganges is increasing, and that Patna itself is likely soon to feel the full weight of the flood – the city's too close to the confluence of the Ganges and the Gandak for comfort, and the Gandak's bringing down any God's amount of water – also there's a long build-up expected from the tidal bore out of the Bay of Bengal. That's expected to be abnormally high. The General has ordered the division to stand by from now for movement at short notice. The first priority is to be the evacuation of the women and children from Patna itself, and that will be ordered immediately acute danger threatens – the General's reluctant to take precipitate action in case he offends the inhabitants—'

'Offends the inhabitants my bottom,' Brora announced in a loud voice. 'Can't they be damn well ordered to evacuate at once?'

'The General has decided not,' Lakenham said coldly.

Brora gave a harsh laugh. 'No doubt against your advice, sir. It would take a blasted idiot *not* to give contrary advice—'

'Thank you for your testimonial, Major,' Lakenham snapped, his colour high, 'but I stand in no need of it. Kindly remain silent at least until I've finished.' In point of fact, Brora had been right: Lakenham's own wish was for an immediate evacuation while there was still time, but Bloody Francis had been adamant that no fences were to be rushed. People did not like being torn from their homes and there might be trouble, he had insisted. To an extent he was right, but the final warning might not come in time; and Patna had nothing like enough boats available for the movement of its huge population by means of the flood-water itself when it came. And when it came, it was likely to be a deluge. Lakenham was about to continue when a noise like bedlam swept suddenly in from the compound, shouts and cries accompanied by the rattle of rifle-fire. Lakenham swung round as Lord Dornoch ran for a window. Before the Colonel had reached it, a dishevelled lance-corporal, minus his helmet and with mud spattered across his face, ran unceremoniously into the mess and approached him.

'Sir—'

'What is it, Corporal Meachin?'

'A mob, sir. A mob's attacking the quarter-guard, sir!'

'And you've opened fire?'

'Over their heads, sir, no more than that.'

Lakenham swore; Bloody Francis would burst a blood-vessel. As Lord Dornoch made for the compound at the rush, Brora's hectoring voice could be heard shouting loudly for Ogilvie.

'Captain Ogilvie! Where's Captain Ogilvie!'

'Here, Major—'

'Get out there, d'you hear me? You have the duty. Get out there and deal with the damn mob at once!'

Ogilvie had already been on his way, pausing only to snatch his Sam Browne and its holstered revolver from a rack outside the mess. He went at the double into the compound, saw the yelling mob crowding the gateway and the quarter-guard under its sergeant standing shoulder to shoulder with rifles at the ready. Stones and filth were being thrown, clearly visible in the light from the guard lantern and from a number of flares held aloft by the mob. The soldiers were already covered with slime and were bleeding where the jagged stones had struck. But discipline was holding firm, and the rifles remained silent after that first warning volley. The mob's attack, however, was now beginning to outflank the gate and the quarter-guard: heads were appearing over the wall, bodies were leaping down into the compound. Ogilvie, running up to join the quarter-guard and add an officer's authority, was only too well aware that the building could be over-run within minutes and, along with Fettleworth himself, overwhelmed in the absence of any more troops.

A moment later, a diversion came.

Two

The Regimental Sergeant-Major had been making his rounds of the cathedral prior to leaving for his billet in the college when the report had reached him of trouble outside.

'There's a mob on the move, sir,' a private reported, 'though it looks like they're passing by, sir.'

'I'll take a shuftee,' Cunningham said, and moved fast for the west door. Once outside, there was no doubt about the mob: what seemed to be thousands of natives were going past, wielding heavy sticks. They were taking no notice of the cathedral or of the picquet: possibly the British God was being respected, possibly the mob's aim lay elsewhere. They were moving under hundreds of flaring torches in the direction of the college where Fettleworth had set up his headquarters. Cunningham went back inside and called the colour-sergeants together.

He said, 'I fancy they're after Division. I intend to march in support – we're the handiest placed of all the battalions.' The rest of the infantry had been billeted over in the far side of the city, away from the college. 'You'll fall the men in, and march them out by companies, Colour MacTrease?'

'Sir!'

'B Company remains behind to mount guard over the cathedral. Remember the orders, all of you: no retaliation unless it's forced upon you.'

The colour-sergeants turned away to pass the orders to their section sergeants and within the minute the great cathedral was echoing to the military commands as the men were hustled from the pews and marched outside to form up. The RSM took the lead of the battalion behind the pipes and drums, and strode out with his wet kilt clinging to his thighs as he moved. The Royal Strathspey marched out right into the mob itself; the natives fell back as they saw the rifles with the gleaming bayonets fixed, the brightly-polished steel reflecting back the red light of the flares. At first the shouting and screaming died away, but there was soon a rising murmur that once again became a bedlam of yelling as the marching men were virtually swallowed up by the native horde. The mob ahead, however, kept up its own advance in front of the pipes and drums, and the battalion was able to move on behind them.

* * *

Outside the government college Major Blaise-Willoughby, the Political Officer attached to Division, lifted a hand and protectively laid it on his pet monkey, Wolseley, perched in its accustomed place on his shoulder, Blaise-Willoughby tilted his head to one side. 'Sounds like your Scots, Ogilvie.'

'It is.'

'Well, I hope they have a care for the orders. We don't want trouble.'

Ogilvie said, 'If you ask me, we've got it already.' He dodged a flung stone, which crashed into the ground behind him. 'There has to come a time when we fight back!'

'Only as a last resort.'

Ogilvie was about to speak again when there was a loud shout from the rear: 'Blaise-Willoughby! Where's that blasted Political feller!' Bloody Francis had appeared, accompanied by Brigadier-General Lakenham; the Divisional Commander was wearing a gilded field service cap, the rest of his uniform being obscured beneath a vast cape that kept the rain at bay. *'Blaise-Willoughby!'*

'Here, sir.'

'Eh? Oh – there you are. Come here.'

Blaise-Willoughby moved across to join his General, one hand steadying Wolseley. Fettleworth glared at the monkey, whom he detested. Stones fell around him, but he stood his ground and thus far remained unhit. 'Tell the buggers to go away!' he said angrily, blowing out his white moustache. 'Tell 'em what we're here for – you have both Pushtu and Urdu, so you ought to penetrate.

'I suggest—'

'Oh, get on with it and don't argue, Blaise-Willoughby.' Fettleworth yelped as a stone glanced off his caped shoulder. 'Get on with it before I become a damn casualty myself!'

Blaise-Willoughby shrugged, cleared his throat, and started shouting towards the mob. The pipes and drums of the Royal Strathspey had been heard by the natives and the clamber over the college wall had stopped. There seemed to be some hesitancy in the air now, and as the shouting lessened Blaise-Willoughby's voice became audible. He spoke for some minutes, while Fettleworth fidgeted impatiently, his face redder than ever in the light from the flares, a redness that contrasted strongly with the white bush of hair on his upper lip.

'Are you achieving anything, Blaise-Willoughby?' Fettleworth called out angrily.

Blaise-Willoughby turned his head. 'Patience, sir, if you please.'

'Oh, balls to patience, Blaise-Willoughby, patience didn't build the Raj, guns did. Not that I want the guns to open,' Fettleworth added hastily. 'Captain Ogilvie?'

Ogilvie turned, and doubled back towards the Divisional Commander. Halting, he saluted smartly. 'Sir?'

'Your Scots. They're not to open fire.'

'No, sir. Mr Cunningham's aware of the orders, sir.'

'Cunningham?'

'The RSM, sir.'

'Yes, I see. Should have said so, I can't remember the names of everyone, can I? Where's your Colonel?'

'Here, sir,' Lord Dornoch said.

'I'd like you to send Captain Ogilvie in person to make certain the order's obeyed, Colonel.'

Dornoch said, 'That's really not necessary, sir. My Sar'nt-Major is—'

'Kindly do as I say, Colonel, and at once.'

Dornoch shrugged and passed the order. Saluting again, Ogilvie turned about and made for the gate and the mob beyond. As he did so, Fettleworth began shouting again at the Political Officer. This time, Blaise-Willoughby, to Fettleworth's fury, took no notice but carried on addressing the mob. By now the van of the Royal Strathspey's advance was close, and the pipes and drums were beating out strongly, subduing the lessened noise from the native hordes: Blaise-Willoughby seemed to be having an effect, representing the strong British presence as the saviour it was intended to be. Ogilvie's own knowledge of the native dialects was good, and he was well able to follow the Political Officer's reassurances in answer to the natives' shouts of fear that the British came to their city with fire and sword, only to add to the terrible threat of the waters of the Ganges. Ogilvie pushed firmly through the mob, his hands ostentatiously behind his back and far from his revolver in its holster. From time to time he was jostled, but that was all. Despite the chill of the downpour, he was sweating profusely into his uniform tunic: it was touch-and-go all the way, in fact. If the natives should decide to do more than jostle, he would be done for. There would be nothing more useless than his revolver; the moment he drew it, he would be torn to shreds. But he kept his expression calm and his eyes level, and he reached the pipes and drums in safety, passing to their rear to make contact with the Regimental Sergeant-Major.

'Well met, Sar'nt Major!' he said, turning to take up the step.

Cunningham said, 'I don't know if I took too much upon myself, Captain Ogilvie, sir, but to stay put—'

'All's well, Sar'nt Major. You're just to bear in mind the orders, that's all – I've been sent by General Fettleworth to tell you so.'

'Aye, sir. The men have behaved well – there's been plenty of provocation but no retaliation other than by word of mouth, as you might say ... and just as well we'd left holy ground behind by that time, sir!'

Ogilvie grinned. As the van of the battalion pushed on, the natives let them through without hindrance. The mob was beginning to desperse now, thanks to Blaise-Willoughby; the natives were streaming past the college gates or fading into the alleys and passages that criss-crossed the city with their festering, open drains and their human dereliction. The pipes and drums fell silent as they passed through the gates into the college compound. They were brought to a halt with the battalion once the rear files had entered. Ogilvie marched forward to report to Lord Dornoch and General Fettleworth. Fettleworth said, 'Major Blaise-Willoughby tells me he's made my intentions clear to the natives. I dare say we'll have no more trouble now, and it's just as well I acted promptly.'

'Yes, indeed, sir,' Dornoch said with his tongue in his cheek. 'What do you wish done with my battalion?'

Fettleworth raised a hand and rasped at his pop-eyed face. 'I shall have to consider. In the meantime, I shall call a conference of all officers. I'll use the college assembly hall. See to that, Lakenham. All officers to assemble immediately.'

'And my battalion?' Dornoch asked remindingly.

Fettleworth hissed with annoyance. 'Oh, blast your battalion, Dornoch, they're soldiers, aren't they? They can wait. Fall them out – no, stand them easy – until I've made my decisions.'

Bloody Francis Fettleworth was not a loved general to his division; although all recognised his personal bravery in action, he was known as a man of turgid mind and a devotee of self-indulgence. How he had ever become a lieutenant-general remained a mystery; it was common knowledge that he was carried by his Chief of Staff and his ADC. In the last resort they usually prevented his putting too many feet wrong. Tonight, he was anathema to the Scots as they remained standing easy in the teeming rain; standing easy meant they could move any part of their bodies other than tongues and feet. But they were Scots and the air was blue with the movement of tongues describing the ancestry of their Divisional Commander. However, their purgatory was short: Lord Dornoch's vehement protests so exacerbated Fettleworth's mind that he snapped, angrily, that for all he cared the Royal Strathspey could go to the devil. Putting his own interpretation on this, Dornoch sent a subaltern to fall out the battalion; thereafter they crowded the kitchens and servants' quarters of the college and did their best to dry themselves out and where possible to purloin some of the viands intended for the officers. Above, in the assembly hall, Fettleworth announced via his Chief of Staff the details of the operation to be mounted to save life in and around Patna. In basis it was simple and straightforward: Fettleworth had now decided upon an evacuation of the women and children at first light next day, since Blaise-Willoughby's words would spread and soothe the natives, and all available men would be required for this prime duty. The women and children were to be shepherded out of the threatened city and moved as far as possible from the likely water-spread of the Ganges. If the waters should overtake them, there would be boats available but unfortunately not in sufficient quantity to shift the whole number of women and children, estimated to be not far short of a hundred thousand souls. When asked about the alternative, Fettleworth replied that the soldiers would have to wade. The women and children would in most cases have carts that could be pushed and might float, and if necessary those carts would have to carry persons rather than possessions; it would be up to each officer, NCO and man to ensure that this happened in an orderly fashion. This was precisely why the division was there; the natives could not be trusted to evacuate themselves without looting and bloodshed and the wholesale abandonment of the weak in favour of household goods. So said Fettleworth, taking over from Lakenham now.

'All battalions,' he announced pompously, 'will be split into companies under their company commanders and will take over areas of the city as allocated on the map.' He tapped a large wall map behind him. 'You must all study this in detail as soon as I've finished. Once the city is clear, then the various battalions will be extended into other areas to the east, covering as much ground as is humanly possible.' He paused. 'I am informed that additional troops are being entrained from Southern Army at Ootacamund, and are coming to my assistance – under Major-General Farrar-Drumm himself, which is a damn nuisance but can't be helped.' Realising too late that he had uttered an indiscretion in disparaging a fellow general, he covered his confusion by bringing out a vast red silk handkerchief and blowing his nose. 'I think that's all for now. You may disperse, gentlemen ... further orders will be notified as necessary, and I, of course, shall be standing by throughout to offer advice. Yes, Dornoch, what is it now?'

'My battalion, sir—'

'Oh, blast your battalion, Dornoch, where did they come from?'

'From the cathedral, sir, where they're billeted.'

'Send them back, then, there's no room for them here.'

Added to by the continuous, torrential rain, the waters of the Ganges, roaring down from their source in the Himalayan ice-cave of Bhagirathi, passing Gangotri in its elevation of 10,319 feet, joined later by the Alaknanda River, had stormed into British India a little above Hardwar. Now they raced towards the city of Patna leaving havoc behind them as they flowed on from previously devastated land. Westwards from Patna everything was flattened and bodies were widespread, bodies that were already rotting and spreading disease. Hundreds of these bodies had in fact been observed under black clouds of vultures from the troop trains as they had chugged eastwards from Peshawar; and during that night urgent orders came from Calcutta via the telegraph wires that troops were to be detailed to move back to the west for corpse disposal and to spread disinfectant under supervision of the medical officers and their orderlies.

When woken with these tidings, Fettleworth was annoyed. 'I haven't the troops to spare, Lakenham,' he said. 'It's one or the other, the dead or the living. Dammit, can't the dead be left to the vultures?'

'Not in Calcutta's view, sir, evidently.'

'Calcutta?' Fettleworth asked vaguely.

'Where the despatch came from, sir.' Lakenham coughed. 'Originated by His Excellency.'

'Ah – His Excellency! Yes, I see. Well, then, we'll have to do it, won't we? You'd better give the necessary orders, Lakenham.'

'Yes, sir. If you'd tell me what your orders are, I shall see that they're transmitted.'

Fettleworth gnawed at the trailing ends of his heavy walrus moustache, his eyes protruding as he cogitated. Then he said, 'Send those Scots. The 114th Highlanders. They're accustomed to bodies ... all over the Highlands, I believe – hard winters and insufficient food, you know. Yes, they'll do. I can't spare more than the one battalion, that's obvious, the living *must* come first.'

'But the living, sir, can quickly become the dead.'

Fettleworth raised his eyebrows. 'What d'you mean by that?'

Lakenham sighed. 'The spread of disease, sir, which is what His Excellency fears. We must back up the 114th's medical officer, must we not, with other medical officers, plus orderlies and supplies?'

'I don't see why. Medical details – from the Civil side, I think – have already moved in where the floods have receded west of us. Isn't that enough?'

'Apparently not in His Excellency's view, sir.'

Fettleworth shifted about angrily in the bed. 'Oh, damn, very well then, see to it, Lakenham. But whatever you do, don't deplete my medical services too far. *I* need leeches too, not that any of them are any good except for administering to the men's bowels.' Fettleworth, having thumped back into his bed, came upright again as his ADC entered his room without knocking. 'Hoity-toity, what's this, Captain Fellowes, have your manners deserted you?'

'I'm sorry, sir—'

'So I should damn well think. Well, what is it now?'

'The river, sir!'

'What about it? I'm aware there's a bloody river, man!'

'Yes, sir. It's rising, sir – rising very fast, sir. Sectors of the city are already under three feet of water, and—'

'The devil they are!' Fettleworth bounced out of bed and stood there in his pyjamas, looking greatly agitated. 'Lakenham, the plan must go into operation at once – *at once*, d'you hear? Women and children – the evacuation's to start now. Rouse out all the infantry, they already have their orders.'

'And the 114th, sir?'

'What about the 114th?'

'Disposal of the dead—'

'Cancelled, Lakenham, for the time being at any rate. Dornoch's to act in compliance with previous orders. Find me a boat. I shall accompany the operation myself, to give cheer to the men.' Fettleworth started to pull on his uniform.

The urgent orders were sent out by runners, and the bugles sounded from Division in brassy confirmation. As the regiments turned out from their billets to be mustered by the NCOs, they found the surging water reaching to their waists in some cases. Patna was like a sea, with many islands where the buildings rose. The air was filled with noises – the shouting of orders, the cries and screams of women and children from the flooded alleys. The stench was appalling as the foetid contents of the open drains were swirled wholesale about the city. Ogilvie, making his way with difficulty to take over his company outside the cathedral, was almost run down by an empty boat floating free on the flood-water; taking a grip, he pulled himself across the gunwale. There were no oars or paddles, but using his hands as a means of propulsion he was able to move faster than on foot: swimming, in the fearsome muck that floated past, was not to be thought of.

A little way farther on, he came across the Colonel and Brora, pushing through the filth, and he hailed them.

Brora turned. 'Praise God,' he said. Thankfully, the two officers clambered in, helped by Ogilvie. They hand-paddled on for the cathedral, where the Royal Strathspey was already mustering under Cunningham. One by one the officers came up, soaked and filthy, stinking to heaven like all else in the stricken city.

Dornoch raised his voice. 'Carry on by companies as detailed. Get to your sectors and do your best. Captain Black?'

'Colonel?' A long, thin figure loomed below a guard lantern.

'Cover all our sectors as best you can, if you please, Captain Black. The Major and I will give ourselves a roving commission as well, and we'll need a runner each.'

'I'll detail them immediately, Colonel.' The Adjutant turned away, plunging back into the gloom of the night and calling for the Regimental Sergeant-Major. By this time Ogilvie had contacted B Company and his colour-sergeant.

MacTrease asked, 'How in heaven's name, sir, do we find the way?'

'To our sector? It's in my head, Colour,

and I'll be the guide.'

'We're still likely to get lost, sir.'

Ogilvie nodded. 'True enough. If we do, then we'll cope with what we find, wherever we happen to be.'

'Aye, sir, that's about all we can do, no doubt.'

Ogilvie passed the word to move out and the files of B Company waded along behind him. There was no vestige of a moon and the only breaks in the otherwise total darkness were the guard lanterns carried by himself as guide and by his colour-sergeant and section sergeants. It was a nightmare progress as they floundered through the water – which, luckily, didn't appear to be deepening any further. All manner of things floated past them, human corpses, dead animals, garbage composed largely of rotting vegetable matter. The corpses were mostly those of old men and women, the ancients unable to get away from the flood's onrush, but there was the occasional child or baby torn, no doubt, from a frantic mother. Natives called from the upper storeys of the dwellings, beseeching help; these had to be ignored, had to be left to the company detailed for the sector. It was hard enough to pass by, especially when young children and babies were seen, thrust forward from the windows by their parents; but the overall plan had to be kept to in the wider interest of the whole population. Moving on, Ogilvie reflected on the vast miseries of the Indian sub-continent, of the appalling gulf between high and low, between enormous, unbelievable wealth and the wretched poverty that led to scavenging for food in the heaps of garbage. Now there wouldn't be even that; the garbage had all succumbed to the widening Ganges. Both human being and pariah dog, those who shared the garbage, would go hungry now, at least until the Supply and Transport columns followed in from Nowshera with their basic food stocks, rice largely, to distribute.

Alongside Ogilvie, MacTrease said, 'The smell, sir. It has the stench of death in it.'

'The bodies...'

'I don't mean them, sir. I mean the disease. Nothing will ever stop the spread, when this is over.'

'Try not to think about it,' Ogilvie advised. 'It's little more of a risk than normal in India.'

'Aye, that's true maybe, sir.'

'It's always been with us, ever since we first came out.'

'Aye, sir.' MacTrease seemed unconvinced; Ogilvie didn't blame him. The bugs of cholera, malaria and dysentery made no distinction between brown skins and white. Once before, the regiment had faced cholera and it had been an appalling experience, with comrades laid out daily for burial in the hard ground of the North-West Frontier. No one wanted to go through that again, and it was true enough that this flood was going to bring a greatly increased danger to the soldiers. Meanwhile they forged on, pushing against the filthy water; after a while the flood's depth seemed to fall away a little, and they could go a little faster. When Ogilvie judged that he was in his allotted sector according to Fettleworth's memorised map, he halted the advance and with MacTrease waded down the company line. Each man, he said, would take as many families as he could shepherd out of the city. There was a need for hurry: even though the water had dropped a little where they stood – and this was merely because they had come to slightly higher ground – the reports had indicated that soon it would deepen fast and the hovels would be completely submerged.

'When you've collected your families,' Ogilvie said, 'we'll muster to the south of the city – there's some high ground that you'll have seen from the train as we came in. If you don't know how to find it, the families will know. If you come across any boats not already being used by other units, commandeer them. Now get to it.'

They did. Spreading out along the alley as

the men and women called down, each man entered a house and tried to make the terrified inhabitants understand that they must trust him to take them to a place of safety. Entering one, Ogilvie found a family of parents, seven children, an aged grandparent and what seemed to be three aunts. They clustered about him, crying, pulling at his uniform, all jabbering together. He made them understand. There was, the father said, a cart at the back of the dwelling, already laden with such household goods as he possessed. The cart, Ogilvie said, must be unloaded and the children and the aged grandmother embarked instead.

'And quickly,' he ordered. 'There may be little time left. If we're lucky, the cart will float on the water.'

They got moving, jabbering without cease as the cart was half pushed, half floated out into the water-filled alley. As they got the children and their grandmother aboard, the cart sank lower and the wheels took the ground. It would be a case of pushing after all, but there were two parents and three aunts to do that. Ogilvie stood guard: there were desperate people around, those taking a risk, unshepherded, against the chances of the water deepening, and these might attempt to crowd the cart, or seize it away for their own use. But as it turned out there was no time for that. Ogilvie with his charges had gone no more than fifty yards along the alley when there was a sudden roaring sound, at first distant but coming very rapidly closer, and a wall of water was seen in the company lanterns, surging high and fast and sweeping smack into the end of the alley between the close-set buildings.

Three

By the time Fettleworth had dressed in his uniform and had arrived with his bugle at the main entrance to the college, the floods had reached the building and the water stood half way up the steps.

Fettleworth wrinkled his nose. 'What a stench to be sure! Where's my Chief of Staff?'

'Here, sir,' Lakenham answered from behind.

'I sent for a boat, did I not?'

'You did indeed, and it's coming across from the gate now.'

'Oh, good.' Bloody Francis stared across the flooded compound, scratching beneath an arm. He was much concerned about his need to scratch: very probably the rising waters had driven all manner of bugs to seek a refuge other than their normal habitat, but just at the moment there was no time to seek assurance from his Divisional Medical Officer. A boat was undoubtedly approaching and could be seen beneath the light from a guttering guard lantern in the bows.

It was a small boat, and was being propelled by oars wielded by a lance-corporal, while a sergeant held the lantern. This craft made a wavering course towards the Divisional Commander, who looked at it with dislike.

'Not large,' he said. 'Not large enough.'

'It was the only one available at short notice, sir.'

'Oh, rubbish, it can't be. However, I suppose it will have to do. I don't want to impede the operation in the smallest way, of course. That lance-corporal looks rather ham-handed, don't you think, Lakenham? What's his regiment?'

'The Manchesters, sir.'

'Make a note to have words with his Colonel,' Fettleworth said. Some thirty seconds later the rowing-boat took the steps with a considerable bump and the sergeant, getting to his feet, fell to the bottom-boards. 'There you are,' Bloody Francis said in disgust. 'What did I tell you, Lakenham? Most unseamanlike.'

'The men are infantrymen, sir!' Lakenham snapped.

'Kindly don't argue, my dear fellow, it's most unbecoming in a Chief of Staff,' Fettleworth said with dignity. He gave a hitch to his stomach and was about to move down towards the boat when a staff-sergeant approached Lakenham, saluted smartly, and handed over a despatch. Lakenham read it quickly then looked up.

'What is it?' Fettleworth asked.

'A message on the telegraph, sir. It comes from the stationmaster at Bundarbar—'

'Bundarbar, where's that, Lakenham?'

'Ten miles back, sir, towards the west.'

'Oh yes, we passed through it. Well?'

'The train from Rawalpindi is marooned there and is flood-bound.'

'I'm most sorry to hear it,' Fettleworth said tartly. 'But why bother division, may I ask?'

'Because it's coming under attack, sir—'

'*Attack?* By natives, Lakenham?' Bloody Francis appeared thunderstruck as Lakenham gave a nod. 'Why, the buggers! It's unbelievable, isn't it, to attack when the Raj is doing all it damn well can to assist in this blasted business!' He paused, wiping at his face and trying to disregard the mounting stink from the flood. 'Or are there only natives aboard the train ... not our own people?'

'Not natives only, sir. The message refers to the Civil side – government Civilians returning from Murree to Calcutta—'

'Bloody fools!' Fettleworth snorted. 'Fancy entraining for the east during a period of damn flood – never heard the like! Typical of Civilians, though. I suppose they're asking for my assistance, are they, well, they can damn well think again. I have my hands full as it is and I'm going to need every man in my command.'

'There is a ring of urgency—'

'Never mind that, Lakenham, how the devil does a damn chi-chi stationmaster think I can get through to them short of swimming I'd like to know—'

'And there are families.' Lakenham's voice had risen to a shout. 'Women and children, sir!'

'What?'

'I think you heard, sir,' Lakenham said grimly. 'Civilian families, plus one military dependant who comes somewhat close to home – a Miss Fiona Elliott, niece of Lord Brora, second-in-command of the 114th—'

'Goodness gracious me!' Fettleworth gaped in concern, but shook his head. 'I'm damn sorry – damn sorry! But there's truly *nothing* I can do at this moment, that's obvious.' Bloody Francis moved on, ponderously, for the rowing-boat, looking grave. It was always the very devil when a military dependant came under threat – the men didn't like it at all and small blame to them. Fettleworth more or less fell into the boat; Lakenham and the bugler followed with greater ease. Fettleworth spoke to the sergeant. 'Row me to the men,' he said. 'I wish to be seen by as many of my men as is possible.'

The sergeant passed the order on and the

lance-corporal, looking overawed at having so important a passenger in his care, bent to the oars. Bloody Francis proceeded across the compound and out through the gate into the city, as if it were a one-man Trooping the Colour ceremony, a rallying-point to be seen by all and never mind the appalling discomfort. As he went, Fettleworth pondered deeply, gnawing at the trailing ends of his moustache. That train in Bundarbar ... it could mean much trouble. Had he been wise, really, to refuse assistance? Families – women and children, and Lord Brora's niece! Brora was a turbulent officer, Fettleworth had heard. And the Civilians ... Civilians were Civilians, the dreadful bane of the military. The Civilians always considered themselves superior, believed themselves, not without truth to be sure, closer than the military to the government, to the Viceroy, to Whitehall – even to Her Majesty, which particular presumption was patent balderdash, of course, since Her Majesty was well known to cherish her soldiers beyond price. Even so. Her Majesty had some care for her Civilians and that should be borne in mind, much as Fettleworth would have liked to see all the Civilians perish. They were a dreadful bunch of clerkly pimps – Under-Secretaries, Government accountants, Salt Department officials, who always thought they were God, customs and revenue, railways, water, census wallahs – bah! Detritus not to be compared with Her Majesty's generals. But powerful, it had to be admitted. It had indeed...

Fettleworth blew through his moustache and glanced sideways at Lakenham, sitting beside him on the foremost thwart of the rowing-boat. Blast Lakenham, it was all his fault, the fellow always managed to push him into a false position simply by the inflexion in his voice. It was always obvious what Lakenham expected him to do, and because of that he always did the opposite. Fettleworth seethed but as yet remained silent. Really, there was nothing he could do about that damn train anyway, as he'd already said. When the waters receded, then he would act. But by that time the train might with luck be able to get moving again, at any rate if the track hadn't had its support washed away, and help might not be needed. Of course, there was the matter of the wretched attacking natives – brigands, no doubt, and possibly even some Thugs with their dreadful strangulation tactics.

Could a battalion advance by swimming? Certainly not for ten miles. Lieutenant-General Fettleworth had just about reached one of his customary panaceas for use in times of stress, which was to display a masterly inactivity until clarity emerged, when there was a shout of alarm from the rowing lance-corporal.

'Hold tight, sir! There's a deluge coming down behind you, sir!'

Fettleworth turned to look over his shoulder: he blenched. A wave like a Cape Horn roller was coming fast, rising high in the confines of the city street, rushing along with its filth and its potential for overwhelming boats ... Fettleworth turned away from it and shut his eyes and a moment later felt himself being lifted, high above the rooftops as it seemed, and moving at immense speed, the speed of an express train, with corpses, moving faster even than the laden rowing-boat, flashing past in alarming numbers.

For a brief moment Ogilvie had felt paralysed, both mentally and physically; then he had reacted and passed the only order that was possible and one, indeed, that had in effect been obeyed by a number of B Company even before it had been given.

'Into the houses, fast as you can ... climb to the roofs!'

The men pushed into the dwellings to right and left; most made it inside, but some did not: those who did not vanished in a maelstrom, a whirl of arms and legs. Ogilvie found himself in a narrow passage that was filling with water; filling rapidly. Reaching a ricketty staircase, he went up at the double to the upper storey. He looked from the glassless window. Below him the waters roared past, already only inches below the sill. Along the alley, to east and west, on his side and the opposite one, the faces of B Company looked out in awe. MacTrease was there, almost opposite Ogilvie's window. Ogilvie was about to call to him when a boat was seen, rushing willy-nilly along on the flood with five men in it: soldiers, and one of them instantly recognisable.

MacTrease recognised him too. He called out, 'That was the General, sir.'

Ogilvie waved in acknowledgement as he watched the boat's headlong progress. It was nearly out of sight when something happened to it. All of a sudden it slewed, coming broadside to the water's movement, probably as some projection caught its bows. It rose up alarmingly, and spilled its occupants. The Divisional Commander must not be lost in B Company's sector; Ogilvie didn't hesitate. He hauled himself through the narrow window and dropped into the flood. He was quickly followed by MacTrease and a Scots private. There was no need to swim: the flood carried them fast, and Ogilvie's prayer was that Bloody Francis wouldn't move faster than the rescue. In the event he did not: he was found wedged and furious in a window, with native women chattering and jabbering sixteen to the dozen within. He was being supported by the Chief of Staff and the lance-corporal. The fourth and fifth men had vanished. Kicking out with his feet, Ogilvie propelled himself towards the window and managed to cling to the frame as the waters tugged at his body.

He said, 'I hope you're all right, sir.'

Fettleworth spluttered. 'Where have you come from?'

'I saw you go past, sir, and—'

'May I enquire who you are?'

'Captain Ogilvie, 114th Highlanders, sir.'

'Ogilvie?' Fettleworth peered through the gloom. 'Ah yes, yes, of course, we've met upon occasions, have we not.' The General's teeth were chattering with the cold of the water. 'And your father – the GOC, no less. And you plunged in to save my life, with no thought for your own, a brave act. Now kindly assist General Lakenham to get me into this house, my boy. Clear the natives away, they're a blasted nuisance, cluttering the window.'

'I think they're trying to help, sir—'

'Nonsense.'

Grinning to himself, Ogilvie spoke a few words to the inhabitants of the house. With the assistance of their willing hands, and with MacTrease and the private who had by now reached the scene, the Divisional Commander was hauled and pushed through the window to land face down on the floor, from which he rose instantly with an expression of distaste on his face, dripping water. Then the Chief of Staff got through. The others followed, bidden in a loud voice to do so by their General.

'Well, Captain Ogilvie, this is a pretty kettle of fish. We can achieve no evacuation in current conditions, can we, Lakenham?'

'I fear not, sir. It's been left too late, obviously.'

'That's not my damn fault, Lakenham—'

'I didn't suggest it was, sir.'

'Then have a care for your tone.' Fettleworth pushed angrily at the natives, who were jostling him and beseeching rescue, confident that miracles would be achieved now that such high-ranking officers of the Raj were so astonishingly close at hand. 'Captain Ogilvie, kindly stop these people pestering me.'

Ogilvie gestured to MacTrease; the natives were shepherded into a corner with soothing words and Fettleworth was able to continue. 'I think the evacuation must be suspended or there will be worse casualties. We must hope the waters rise no higher, that's all. With any luck, they will not, They may pass on now to other areas to the east.'

'And Division must follow, sir,' Lakenham said.

Fettleworth removed some debris from his

soaked uniform. 'What's that?'

'Those were the orders, sir: to follow on.'

'Yes, yes, yes I'm aware of that, thank you. However, at the moment I can do nothing about it, since I'm damn well marooned.' Fettleworth stared about the room, at filthy walls and rotting hangings. 'By God, Lakenham, this is a fine setting for Division – which for the time being it must be regarded, I suppose! A fine setting, and I'd be obliged if someone would get me out of it as fast as possible. Where's that lance-corporal – Manchesters, wasn't he?'

'Yessir!' The lance-corporal slammed to attention and saluted. 'Here, sir.'

'Ah. And your boat? Where is *that*?'

'Gone, sir.'

'Gone, did you say?'

'Yessir. Torn away by the flood, sir.'

'Well,' Fettleworth said with surprising mildness, 'I must confess I feared so and I shall not blame you in the circumstances. But what am I to do, Lakenham?'

Lakenham shrugged; there was a glint in his eyes. 'Wait for the waters to recede, sir. There's nothing else you can do, 'pon my soul there isn't!'

Throughout the night the waters remained high and tumultuous and did not recede. When dawn came, pale and wet in a gloomy, rain-filled sky that spoke of yet more floods to come soon, they had still not receded. Fettleworth sat on a dirty, broken-down *charpoy* which he was convinced was filled, as to its straw palliase, with disease and fleas, perhaps even lice though so far he had failed to spot one. Lakenham sat with him, while Ogilvie, MacTrease, the lance-corporal and Private Barber sat on the floor. In a corner the native inhabitants huddled, looking the picture of woe. If the great Lieutenant-General Sahib from Nowshera was unable to save them from their plight, they were doomed indeed and the Raj had feet of clay after all. Fettleworth kept giving them forbearing looks and periodically ordered Ogilvie to silence their wearisome jabbers. His wish had been to chuck them out but he knew he couldn't do that, since short of death there was nowhere to send them to: the native dwellings didn't run to more than one room up and one down, by and large. There was always the roof, of course, but Bloody Francis had a streak of humanity and the roof would be a cheerless and unsafe place. So the natives remained to befoul temporary Divisional HQ. If only his blasted bugler hadn't drowned, some sort of contact might have been made with the outside world and he might have been rescued, but it was no use pondering on what he hadn't got. There must be more boats around, many more boats, but none hove in sight. Fettleworth muttered to himself and pulled never-endingly at his moustache. Damn his wet clothing! It was hideously uncomfortable, and unsafe too. He had in fact removed his uniform but refused to remove his underclothing in front of other ranks and native women, nor would he allow any of the others to do so. He shivered like a castanet. Alongside him Lakenham closed his eyes as if in sleep, and Fettleworth brought him up sharply.

'We need our full alertness, Lakenham. Who knows what may happen?'

'Suppose we take it in turns to sleep?'

'No.'

The weary, wet hours passed. Fettleworth flapped his arms around his thickened body, squelching a dribble of foul water from his vest. Malaria – now, that was a very nasty thing! Fettleworth believed it came from damp conditions, from remaining too long in wet clothing; but without a leech to ask he couldn't really be certain. Then there was cholera, but it was better not to think about that. Now that his underclothing, and his skin, was wet, the itch beneath his arm had stopped, and that was odd too. Fettleworth pondered on it: it could mean that the itch had not been due to bugs after all, and that left disease unless the bugs had simply drowned, but what disease remained a mystery. If only there was a leech! The

Divisional Commander grew colder and colder and as he grew colder he became more alarmed about his possible condition. It was never a good thing to remain wet, malaria or no. He had heard that seamen were frequently wet through for long periods, but salt water didn't hurt one – he knew that. Flood-water was quite different. And if he should die, that fool Lakenham would take over. Then there would be catastrophe, but at least *he* couldn't be blamed.

Soon there were heavy snores as the Divisional Commander, in disregard of his own precept, slept. Lakenham stared bleakly from the rough window as the watery sun did its best to penetrate. He got up to look out: the water was still as high as ever, and with malice aforethought Lakenham woke Bloody Francis to tell him so.

'God!' Fettleworth said, waking with a start as Lakenham shook him by the shoulder. 'What was that?'

'I, sir, your Chief of Staff. The situation hasn't changed, and it is coming towards noon.'

Fettleworth grunted, sat up, and stretched arms and legs. 'My division will be wondering where the deuce I am,' he said complainingly. He joined Lakenham at the window, and looked out, his expression morose. The waters were moving still, really lashing along and still carrying an immense amount of debris including more bodies, but there was not a boat in sight. Faces stared from the other windows in the alley, among them the Scots of Ogilvie's company, and, looking at them. Fettleworth ruminated on another aspect of his responsibilities. There was that confounded railway train, flood-bound in Bundarbar station. God alone could tell what the attacking natives had wrought by this time; with luck, they might have been swept away by the rushing water, but that could not, of course, be relied upon.

Fettleworth turned. 'Captain Ogilvie?'

'Sir?'

'I have orders for you, orders that I cannot pass through your Colonel since he is not here.' Fettleworth bent to his uniform tunic and brought out his handkerchief. He blew his nose violently: he felt as though he had a cold coming on already. 'As you know, the division is under orders to move easterly once I have got away from this blasted hovel and dealt with the aftermath of the present flood. Your company, however, will march the other way – westerly, to Bundarbar.' Fettleworth explained about the marooned train and the presencc aboard it of Lord Brora's niece. Ogilvie was much concerned to learn about Fiona Elliott, who had spent some while in Peshawar on a visit to her uncle before leaving with her mother for Murree some days before the division had been ordered out; she and Ogilvie had become good friends, possibly more than that in spite of Brora's cold opposition ... but Fettleworth was going on and he was obliged to pay attention: '... families, don't you know. You'll march as soon as conditions permit, which I trust will be soon now.' He turned to Lakenham. 'We must not waste time,' he said. 'You and I shall prepare fresh plans to clean the city up. Sanitary details – burial parties – temporary accommodation for those flooded from their homes – food and fresh water if we have enough pending the arrival of the Supply and Transport. A tall order, Lakenham, but the Raj will cope.' He paused, aware of Lakenham's forbearing look. '*Now* what is it?'

'The earlier orders from Calcutta, sir. You intended despatching the 114th back to the west for corpse disposal and to spread disinfectant. Do you remember?'

'Yes, of course I do,' Fettleworth answered angrily. 'I was coming to that. Captain Ogilvie, you will after all rejoin your regiment and march west with them, but at a suitable moment you will detach your own company to the assistance of the Civilians in Bundarbar. If I have no chance to pass the orders to Lord Dornoch in the meantime, you will apprise him of them yourself. Is that clear, Captain Ogilvie?'

In mid-afternoon the water-level began, however imperceptibly, to drop; the speed of flow diminished and by 5 p.m. there was a very distinct improvement. By this time, too, the rain had ceased and the skies had begun to clear. Within a couple of hours it was possible for the troops to leave the shelter of the houses, and Fettleworth, announcing his intention to return to his headquarters in the government college, descended to ground level and stepped outside into an eighteen-inch slop of foul water. Now in possession of detailed orders for Lord Dornoch, Ogilvie mustered his company and marched them off for the cathedral. The count had shown seven men missing, swept away on the flood the night before. Even in peace, British soldiers gave their lives for India and the Raj. Arriving at the cathedral, Ogilvie found that A and E Companies had reported in, having suffered experiences similar to his own. During the evening the remaining companies marched in with the Adjutant; and shortly after this the Colonel and Lord Brora arrived to take the reports from the company commanders. Ogilvie passed Fettleworth's orders to Lord Dornoch; Brora's face suffused when he heard that his niece was aboard the train at

Bundarbar.

'What the devil's she doing there, Ogilvie?'

'I don't know, Major.'

Brora took a pace forward, his eyes furious. An arm came up, threateningly. 'Is this to do with you, damn you? Have you—'

'It's nothing to do with me, Major. I imagine Miss Elliott is on her way to Calcutta for a visit—'

The Colonel cut in speedily. 'We'll not discuss the whys and wherefores now,' he said, giving the Major a hard look. 'We must act. Since the flood's passed through Patna, one would assume it to have passed through Bundarbar as well. The train may be in motion again for all we know if the track's not too much damaged – or it may be under siege.' He sighed. 'I'd have wished to rest the men, but I can't lose time now. You must prepare to move out at once, Major.'

Brora gave a perfunctory salute and turned away with Andrew Black, calling for the Regimental Sergeant-Major. With no more than half-an-hour's stand-easy and a drink of hot cocoa brewed up by the field kitchen before it was packed away for the march, the Royal Strathspey fell in by companies and was moved out westerly through the dereliction of Patna with its slimy mud, its stench and its sad corpses. Before they had left the cathedral precinct a medical detachment had come in with its wagons and carts, three doctors of the Army Medical Staff, a dozen medical orderlies, and a consignment of disinfectants – ammonia, carbolic, formaldehyde, potassium permanganate, lysol, chloride of lime, terebene and corrosive sublimate. As in the case of the human enemy, disease had to be fought with an arsenal. As Lord Dornoch remarked, this was a lesson the army was only just beginning to learn.

'Namby-pambyism,' Brora snapped. 'In the past, we put up with disease, and the fittest survived. We shall all grow soft, Colonel, and the men will become damn walking pharmacies!'

'At least they'll live to fight again,' Dornoch said mildly. 'We've lost too many good men to disease – and not least from our own battalion in the past. You'd do well to remember that.'

'And another thing,' Brora went on, taking no notice of the Colonel's words. He waved his riding-crop towards the medical wagon-line. 'When all that disinfectant garbage is distributed, by God, we shall all smell like the public lavatories at Waterloo station!' He didn't seem, Dornoch thought, over concerned about his niece.

By the early hours of next morning, the battalion was well clear of the city and Surgeon-Major Corton, who was to co-ordinate the corpse disposal and disinfecting of living persons and dwellings in the villages as they passed through, reported to the Colonel that he would begin his operations immediately after dawn. After receiving this report, Lord Dornoch passed the word down the line of march for Captain Ogilvie to attend upon him.

Ogilvie rode forward through the darkness and saluted. 'Colonel!'

'Ah, James. It's time you broke off for Bundarbar. The railway line's over there.' Dornoch pointed to the right of the line of advance. 'I suggest you pick up the track and remain on it – just in case the train gets away, though I fear that in fact the floods may have damaged the line.'

'Yes, Colonel.'

'If the train's still in Bundarbar, your orders will be to remain with it through to Patna and then report to Division and place yourself at General Fettleworth's disposal until the rest of the battalion returns. If the track's impassable, you'll still stay with the train pending further orders and a repair gang from Patna—' The Colonel broke off as Brora thrust his horse forward and rudely interrupted.

'And my niece? What about my niece, Colonel? Is she to be left to the tender damn mercies of Captain Ogilvie and his attempts at amours? Is she—'

'Thank you, Major, that will do.' Dornoch's face was livid. He detected, in Brora's outburst, not so much concern as sheer vindictive rage at Ogilvie's being permitted near his niece even in a defence capacity. 'I have my orders from General Fettleworth and I have every confidence in Captain Ogilvie—'

'You—'

'My orders stand and you will keep silent.' Dornoch turned to Ogilvie. 'Detach as soon as you're ready – and the best of luck, James.'

'Thank you, Colonel.' Ogilvie hesitated: the enmity of Lord Brora could be felt like a knife in the back. 'There's one thing, if I may ask it—'

'Go on.'

'May I take Mr Cunningham, Colonel?'

'H'm. Any particular reason?'

'Only that we're moving into action, Colonel, and—'

'And the Sar'nt-Major's forte is war, James! Well, I don't disagree – I fail to see Mr Cunningham coming to terms with potassium permanganate! Yes, you may take him.'

Thanking the Colonel once again, Ogilvie brought his horse round and rejoined B Company after a word with the Regimental Sergeant-Major, who was delighted with his orders. Ten minutes later B Company had detached, taking with it two pipers and two drummers and a Maxim gun section, the gun itself dismantled and its component parts strapped to the mules. By the time the dawn had lightened the sky, they had reached the railway line. The Colonel's hypothesis was proved correct: the ground had been washed away from the sleepers, and the line had sunk and lay twisted and useless for much of its visible length. It would take large repair gangs and much time before the track could be used again; but Ogilvie kept his line of march alongside the railway, which offered the fastest route to Bundarbar, and time was short now. More than twenty-four hours had passed since word of the attack had reached Division, and there was no knowing what the Scots might find on arrival.

Cunningham was pessimistic. 'The bandits will have plenty of men and guns handy, Captain Ogilvie. They're never short of either! It'll have been a case of attrition of the train's passengers, I don't doubt.'

Ogilvie nodded. A stationary train was a very sitting target indeed. No one would be easier to pick off than its occupants. And as the march continued at forced pace beyond the watery dawn, and the collection of hovels that formed the small town of Bundarbar came up ahead, the Scots heard the sound of the rifles going into action.

Four

The advance was across open country: it was too much to hope that they might remain unseen for long, and they were not. The bandits' attack seemed to be a strong one, judging from the number of smoke puffs from the rifles around the train, which was halted a hundred yards or so east of the station as though an attempt had been made to pull away. As the Scots moved forward, there was a lull in the firing and then the rifles ahead opened up again, this time directed towards the British force.

'Hold your fire!' Ogilvie called. 'Mr Cunningham, break ranks and spread the men out in line.'

'Aye, sir—'

'I'm going to try an encircling movement. One half-company north of the track, the other south, advancing together.'

'Very good, sir.' Cunningham passed the orders to the colour-sergeant and section sergeants, and the company split up, moving on at a crouching run. Ogilvie saw a face appear at one of the train's windows; the face was seen by a bandit as well. A rifle opened; the aim was true, and the face seemed to disintegrate. Cursing, Ogilvie rode on. As the two-sided advance came within a couple of hundred yards of the coaches, Ogilvie shouted the order for the Scots to return the bandits' fire, which so far had caused no more than a handful of flesh wounds. As the Scots rifles opened at close range from both flanks at once, a chance return shot from the bandits took Ogilvie's horse, which crashed under him. Scrambling up, Ogilvie saw that the animal was in pain, badly wounded in the chest, and there was only the one thing to do: he put a bullet in the horse's brain and turned back to the fight. Native bodies were falling fast, throwing up their arms. Then in small groups they began a dash into the surrounding country and as demoralisation set in Ogilvie called the order to fix bayonets and charge. That did it; as the shining steel moved in at the double, with the highland soldiers shouting wildly, the remaining bandits wavered, then broke and fled before a single bayonet found a target. Yelling, pursued by the Scots rifles until Ogilvie passed the word to cease firing, they vanished over some rising ground.

'Round one to us,' Ogilvie said to his senior subaltern, Henry Harrington. 'Not too bad!'

'They'll be back, James. This is just the start.'

'I know. But it gives us the initial advantage all the same. Get everyone aboard the train, Henry, fast as you can.' Ogilvie dashed sweat from his eyes. 'Now we stand by for a siege!'

Fiona was safe. So far, so good. She was the first of the passengers to greet Ogilvie as he clambered aboard after reconnoitring the line back beyond the station, where he had found the telegraph line cut and the station-master dead in his office. To Ogilvie's embarrassment Fiona took him in a tight clasp and kissed him. 'Thank God!' she said when she let him go. 'You of all people, James!'

'Are you all right?' he asked

'Yes—'

'And Lady Mary?' Lady Mary Elliott was Fiona's mother and Brora's sister-in-law, a pleasant enough woman with whom Ogilvie got on well. 'I hope she isn't taking it too badly, Fiona?'

'Oh, mother's all right too,' she said, and added, 'I'm surprised Uncle David let you come!'

'He had no option,' Ogilvie said, smiling.

'But he didn't like it?'

'He didn't like it at all,' Ogilvie answered. 'But more of that later.' He turned to an important-looking Civilian, an elderly man who seemed to have taken command of the train upon himself, judging from his autocratic manner. Muttering some uncomplimentary words about women and damned dalliance, he laid hold of Ogilvie's arm.

'Now look here, young man,' he said from beneath a walrus moustache not unlike Fettleworth's, 'my name's Wilberforce.' He paused as though the name should mean something; it did not. 'Indian Civil. Public Works, Calcutta.'

Ogilvie nodded. He had something of a social climber to deal with, he fancied; Public Works was not, strictly speaking, a part of the exclusive Indian Civil Service, even if it was sometimes referred to as such, mainly by its own people. He introduced himself, adding that he and his company of Scots had been sent by order of Lieutenant-General Fettleworth, currently in Patna.

'So I assumed, Captain Ogilvie,' Wilberforce said. 'I am aware of the military dispositions in this unfortunate flooding. What I want to know is, are any more soldiers being sent?'

Ogilvie shrugged. 'Not so far as I know, but—'

'One company is not enough in my opinion. We have come under attack at times by a force of some three or four hundred men.' Wilberforce's voice shook a little. 'We have many dead, and many more wounded. We have survived – some of us – for this long. I fail to see how we can last much longer.'

Ogilvie said, 'Frankly, I'm surprised that so large a force as you mentioned hasn't rushed the train by now, and taken it. I—'

'They've tried,' Wilberforce said. 'We were provided with an escort of soldiers from Murree ... they did noble work, but they have all been killed. The men among the passengers have made good use of their rifles since then, but it will not be long before the bandits realise that we're defenceless ... or would have been,' he added hastily, 'until your arrival.'

Ogilvie said, 'They've met us once. They may not be so keen to attack now, Mr Wilberforce.'

'But you see, the trouble is, my dear Captain Ogilvie...' Wilberforce's voice trailed away. 'Ogilvie. There is an Ogilvie commanding in Murree ... I wonder—'

'My father.'

'Really?' Wilberforce almost bent his tall body in two, and smiled unctuously, rubbing his hands together. 'So famous a father ... well, well! I am most glad to meet you, Captain Ogilvie, most glad. But as I was about to say, the trouble is, we cannot move. We have no steam and we have no coal – the bandits removed all that was left in the tender, no doubt so as to immobilise us – and in any case the engine-driver and the fireman were killed in the very first attack and—'

'And the line's impassable farther east, I'm afraid. Also back to the west ... just beyond the station. You must have got through only a short time before the sleepers were washed away.'

Wilberforce looked glum. 'I expected it might be impossible to go farther east, of course. I didn't realise the line was gone behind us. You see what we're faced with, Captain Ogilvie?'

'Of course I do, but I'm not too depressed. General Fettleworth won't forget us, you know! If no word comes through about the train, I've no doubt at all he'll send reinforcements, and—'

'But how long?' Wilberforce was almost wringing his hands. 'For one thing there is the question of food. We have very low stocks, even though I have instituted a rationing system, and as for water, we have practically none. It's vital we get supplies in – not least, medical necessities, Captain Ogilvie.'

'Is there sickness?'

Wilberforce shook his head. 'As yet, I'm glad to say, no. It may come. I was referring to bullet wounds. We have many men who have been hit. Some have died since, others will do so unless we have medical attention brought to them. And of course there is the question of the dead ... you will have noticed, I am certain, Captain Ogilvie.' Ogilvie had indeed noticed the dreadful smell that pervaded the train; it was impossible not to be aware of it. 'We haven't been able to – er – dispose of them. Any sign of anyone leaving the train has brought a fresh attack, and there was in any case no possibility of decent burial in the flood water.'

Ogilvie nodded; he asked, 'Is there any special reason why the train was attacked, d'you think? I mean, what with so widespread a flood ... I'd have thought the natives would have other things on their minds – even the bandits.'

Wilberforce looked surprised. 'You don't know, Captain Ogilvie? Was not General Fettleworth informed?'

'Informed of what?'

Wilberforce looked somewhat furtively to right and left before answering. Then, as though instinctively, he lowered his voice. He said, 'We have a cargo, Captain Ogilvie. I was not myself informed until the person in charge of it was wounded, but I would have thought General Fettleworth ... however, no matter. He was not informed, it seems—'

'Or didn't inform me if he was.'

'No. But I think you must be told now. I think that is only fair.' Wilberforce paused, weightily. 'We carry bullion, Captain Ogilvie. Gold bars ... one hundred thousand pounds' worth.' For a moment he watched the effect of this on Ogilvie: a hundred thousand pounds was indeed a lot of money and very well worth the bandits' while – worth a good many bandits' lives as well. Wilberforce went on, 'The consignment, in wooden boxes each containing four bars, is in the guard's van.'

'And the escort – this was chiefly for the bullion?'

'Yes. But as I've told you, all the soldiers have been killed.'

'The bullion's going where – Calcutta?'

'Yes. There was a good deal of secrecy, of course, but somehow or other the bandits have found out – they must have done, I think, or the attacks would not have come in such strength and with such devilish ferocity.' For the first time Ogilvie noticed the shake in Wilberforce's hands; he had been under great strain, as indeed all the passengers would have been; Ogilvie felt he and his Scots had arrived only just in time to provide some much needed moral, as well as physical, support. 'It's never difficult for secrecy to become breached, Captain Ogilvie. We all rely so much upon the natives, who may be loyal and who may not be.'

Ogilvie nodded. 'That's India, as I've come to learn! We'll give your bullion all the protection possible, Mr Wilberforce, and the passengers as well, of course. In the meantime – and most importantly – there's something else, isn't there?'

'What is that, Captain Ogilvie?'

Quietly Ogilvie answered, 'The dead. They'll bring disease. The bodies must be disposed of as a matter of extreme urgency.'

B Company was distributed to Ogilvie's orders throughout the four coaches of the train and a section was detailed to guard the gold bullion in its twenty plain boxes, oblong in shape and immensely heavy. After this Ogilvie had a word with the Regimental Sergeant-Major.

'Coal, Sar'nt Major,' he said.

'Coal, sir? There is none in the tender. I have checked, Captain Ogilvie.'

Ogilvie nodded. 'I know. But I suspect there may be stocks back in the station.' He waved towards the primitive station buildings a little westward of the train. 'What d'you think?'

'I think it would be usual for the station to keep replenishments, Captain Ogilvie, yes.'

'So do I. We must have some of it, Sar'nt-Major, and now is as good a time as any – the natives have vanished for the time being, and there's an urgent need of coal.'

'But the train'll not move far, sir. The track is—'

'I'm not thinking of moving,' Ogilvie

broke in. 'I don't like what I'm going to suggest, but it's vital in the interest of health. The bodies ... they'll have to be burned in the engine furnace, Mr Cunningham. There's no other way, what with the danger of attack and the flood itself.'

Cunningham lifted his head and scratched beneath his jaw. 'It's nasty, sir, very nasty. Would they not float away on the flood, do you think?'

'I doubt it, and anyway the battalion was ordered out to prevent the spread of disease, not add to it. We must still have a care for the loyal native subjects of the Raj, Sar'nt-Major!'

'Aye, the loyal ones,' Cunningham said sounding dour. Ogilvie had spoken lightly, but the RSM was not amused. 'Is this an order you are giving. Captain Ogilvie?'

'Yes, Sar'nt-Major. I'm sorry, but it's unavoidable in my view.'

'Then it will be done, sir. I'll have parties detailed to fetch coal if available, though the Lord knows what they're going to fetch it in, for I do not.' The RSM paused, frowning. Then he said, 'There's maybe a better way, sir.'

'What's that?'

'Unhook the coaches, sir, and have all fit men out on the track to push them one by one back into the railway station, then hook on again and load the tender.'

'*Can* that be done, d'you think?'

Cunningham said, 'If it can't be, Captain Ogilvie, I'll hand in my warrant. We have men enough and drill-sergeants to galvanise them. Aye, it'll be done if you give the word, sir.'

'Right! Consider it given, Sar'nt-Major. You'd better post picquets to give an immediate alarm if the bandits come in while we're working the train along.' Ogilvie nodded. 'Carry on, if you please, Mr Cunningham.'

Cunningham slammed to the salute and turned about. Dropping down to the track, he marched away, right arm swinging, left arm bent to grasp the cane held rigid beneath it, voice raised to summon the section sergeants under Colour-Sergeant MacTrease. Ogilvie turned back into the coach to find Fiona Elliott behind him. He smiled at her, and took her hand. She gave him a rather cold look.

'I heard some of what you were saying to your Sergeant-Major,' she said. 'I think it's horrible.'

'But necessary.'

'It's the sort of thing Uncle David would do.'

'If the Major gave the order, it would be the right one, Fiona, believe me.'

She said, 'The military mind is pretty rotten, if you ask me. Some of those men have – had – wives aboard the train. And children. What are they going to think, James? Isn't it going to be awful for them?'

'It's awful for me too, as a matter of fact,' Ogilvie said, his face hard. 'Don't make it worse. What I've ordered was inevitable. You've not been long enough in India to know what the climate can do, and you've not faced disease. Things spread like lightning, and soon get out of control. As you may have overheard me saying to the Sar'nt-Major, we're not here to add to it. I'm sorry, Fiona, and I really mean that, but it's got to be done.' He added on a softer note, 'Just keep well out of the way and try not to think about it.'

She let out a long breath and for a moment looked away across the desolation of the flooded land, at the hovels of Bundarbar standing out from the water, at the bridge that spanned the Ganges river. Then she turned back and took Ogilvie in her arms, gripping his body with surprising strength as though she would never let go. He felt the shake that was in her and felt her tears on his face. Bringing out his handkerchief he wiped the tears away and smiled down into her eyes. 'It's been bad, hasn't it,' he said. 'But don't worry. Division knows where we are—'

'That old Fettleworth?'

Ogilvie grinned. 'He's not so bad. When

he can tear himself away from thoughts of the Queen at Balmoral, of Windsor, he has a care for his soldiers, Fiona.'

She made a vulgar noise; she was bucking up already, much to Ogilvie's relief. She said, 'Let's talk about something even nastier. Let's talk about Uncle David! What did Uncle do in the great flood, James?' She added bitterly, 'Got drowned, with any luck!'

'How you love him, don't you!'

'You too.'

'He's the Major—'

'And you're his loyal Captain. Don't be so bloody stuffy, James.' Ogilvie felt a start of astonishment at the word bloody; not a word often used by mem'sahibs and one that neither the Major nor her mother, Lady Mary Elliott, Brora's sister-in-law, would have cared to hear from her lips. But Fiona was high spirited and mettlesome and had her own ways of expressing herself and had no liking for the conventions or for the restrictions imposed on young ladies by society in India, which could be narrow-minded in the extreme and never mind the dalliance that went on often enough when husbands were away on active service. That, among the married people, was a different story. Unmarried young ladies were watched with a hawk-like determination by parents and chaperons. And Lord Brora was one of the hawks, acting *in loco parentis* for his dead brother, and a dangerous hawk at that in his other capacity as second-in-command of Ogilvie's battalion. Ogilvie shrugged at the accusation of stuffiness; women had never understood or appreciated a soldier's duty and loyalties. But there was no time now to ponder on such matters: already the dispositions were being made to shift the coaches. While B Company of the Royal Strathspey piled out onto the track, and a section was detailed to split in half and give cover on both sides of the train, the male passengers, or such of them as were fit and young enough to lend a hand, were urged out of the coaches by the persuasive voice of the Regimental Sergeant-Major.

'Come along now, if you please, gentlemen! Lend a hand for your ladies' sake, and for the bairns! Come along now and show me what you're made of. I'll want no slackness, gentlemen, mind that—' Cunningham broke off as a willowy young man protested volubly. 'What is it, sir?'

'I say, this is a bit thick, isn't it? I'm from the India Office in Whitehall, I'm not some damn navvy—'

'Neither am I, sir, I am the Regimental Sergeant-Major of the 114th Highlanders, the Queen's Own Royal Strathspey. Sir! I shall push with the rest – and so will you.'

'What damned—'

'I am not accustomed to be *argued* with, sir, in the execution of my duty. You will be man enough to get down to the track, and you will *push*, sir. *Do you hear me?*'

Scarlet in the face, the young gentleman from Whitehall turned about and did as he was told, his nose high in the air. Cunningham, catching a mutter about a report being made to the Secretary of State, turned his attention to the others; there was no further argument. Ogilvie jumped down, looked back at Fiona, and gave her a smile and his advice to keep inside and keep her head down in case of an attack by the bandits. He walked forward to where two privates were throwing off the coupling of the last coach. MacTrease, in charge of the pushing party, loudly encouraged them to their best efforts; and slowly, grindingly, the wheels began to turn. When the coach had rolled back into the station, MacTrease doubled his party, soldiers and passengers, back to the next to be moved. Throughout the manoeuvre, the Scots picquets on either hand kept watch for any attack, but so far at any rate the natives were not to be seen. Cunningham remarked on this; it was strange, he said, that the bandits were not taking their chance while all the men were in the open and offering a fine target.

'It's no longer such an easy option. Sar'nt-Major!'

'It is not, sir, that's true. All the same, they have immense strength of numbers available.'

'Which they'll use the moment they're ready,' Ogilvie said. 'And I hope that by that time General Fettleworth will have reinforced us, though I'm not banking on it.'

'Not, sir?'

Ogilvie shook his head. 'He'll have other things on his mind. He's under orders to push east towards Calcutta, in the wake of the floods.'

'Aye, sir, I know. But troops are on their way up from Southern Army as I understand it.' Cunningham paused reflectively. 'Major-General Farrar-Drumm, sir ... he's a very old gentleman indeed – of course, you know that.'

'A brave fighter, whatever his age, Sar'nt-Major.'

'Yes. I remember that, sir, from the rout of that Star of Islam's force.' Cunningham gave a cough. 'With every respect for a brave old gentleman, his ideas are fixed back in the Crimea and the Zulu war. I think he'll not prove to be as keen on succour and sanitation as on fighting, sir.'

'I don't follow, Sar'nt-Major ... that is, not entirely. He's scarcely likely to mount a charge on the flood survivors, I fancy!'

'No, sir, indeed not. But—'

'And he's being entrained for Patna so far

as I know. Not Bundarbar.'

'Quite, sir. But things can alter fast in India. It's known at Division that General Fettleworth finds General Farrar-Drumm an irritation. It crosses my mind that General Fettleworth may suggest that General Farrar-Drumm should march to our relief, sir, and thus kill two birds with one stone.'

Ogilvie laughed, and, using the Regimental Sergeant-Major's nickname, said, 'Bosom, I think you're being a professional pessimist! It's scarcely likely that General Fettleworth will reinforce us by more than a battalion at the most – and that wouldn't call for the presence of the Southern Army Commander in person!' He turned his attention back to the work in hand; this was proceeding at an unexpectedly fast pace and it was not long before the last of the coaches was being pushed into the station and followed up by the engine and tender, the latter handily placed to receive the coal stocks. MacTrease made his way along the track, supervising the re-coupling of the coaches, while Ogilvie and his subalterns, with the RSM, mustered the soldiers and the highly-placed Civilians for the back-breaking task of humping the coal, by hand and shovel, from the dump to the tender. After only some fifteen minutes' labour, watched from the train's windows by the women and children, every man was black with the coal-dust and resembled the company of one of Her Majesty's ships of war coaling at Gibraltar or Aden.

But the worst part was yet to come: everyone aboard the train knew by this time what the purpose of loading the coal was. True, once the repair gangs from Patna had relaid the railway line, coal would be needed to give steam to the engine; but by that time they would probably need to coal again. The many dead would consume much fuel in their burning. However, the time for that had not come yet: the tender was almost filled when the alarm was given by the picquets on both flanks simultaneously, and Ogilvie saw the hordes of bandits sweeping in and heard the discharges of *jezails* fitted with long, snaky bayonets, the weapons especially beloved of the Pathan tribesmen from the Frontier. Seeing the turbaned heads and bearded faces, Ogilvie realised, with a sinking heart, that it was not just the local banditry he had to contend with.

Five

There was, as ever, many a true word said in jest; or if not in this case jest, then many a gloomy if hypothetical prognostication that was destined to come woefully true. Dire misfortune was to blame: Major-General Sir Clarence Farrar-Drumm had had an abominable run of luck. His railcade out of Ootacamund by way of Coimbatore, Salem and the Eastern Ghats, Secunderabad and many, many other points north on its immensely long haul to Patna, had, when it reached the flood areas, become split up on account of the water everywhere to be seen. Eventually Farrar-Drumm, with his staff and his Vigor's Horse-Action Saddle – as used by Her Royal Highness the Princess of Wales – to keep his rheumatic body fit, had become detached from the main rail transport of Southern Army and had been shuffled off into a siding by an apparent mistake on the part of an Indian railwayman. Here he sat in angry but impotent state together with his Chief of Staff, his ADC, his brigade commanders and his departmental chiefs from the medical staff, the signals, the ordnance and the Supply and Transport – for he had decided not to travel, as it were, too light, leaving behind in Ootacamund only the great guns of the horse and field artillery and the cavalry units of his command, the latter with much reluctance.

'Blasted nuisance, all this,' he complained to his Chief of Staff.

'Yes, indeed, sir.'

'Somebody ought to be shot.'

This needed no answer and it got none. After some minutes of aggrieved silence, Farrar-Drumm began again. Hoarsely he asked, 'Are we in that feller Fettleworth's area yet, or are we not?'

'We are, sir.'

'Then somebody ought to shoot Fettleworth.'

They sat on, scarlet-clad and gilded, assailed by flies and smell. Peace lay over the land – peace and water, and utter silence, a nasty brooding silence. Farrar-Drumm fidgeted; he didn't like Northern India, didn't like it at all. The whole ambience, the very atmosphere, was different from the South and dear old Ootacamund – Ooty was so very English, with its tea-parties, its dances and dinner-parties and its gossip, not to mention the concerts in the bandstand with the music played by the regimental bands. No doubt Simla was little different, that he was prepared to admit, but this wretched place in which he was marooned was not Simla by a very long chalk. It was a detestable place, really just a railway siding and that was all – rather like Crianlarich in Argyllshire but without the backdrop of the mountains. After seething and fuming for a while General Farrar-Drumm announced, from behind a veritable forest of white hair that grew like bushes upon head and face, though the chin itself was bare, that he was about to use his thunderbox, but not upon the train.

'Need to stretch my legs, doncher know.' He pointed through the train window with his walking-stick. 'There's some highish ground, clear of the blasted water. Bring my half-wellingtons and send for *my sepoys* – they'll have to bring my tent as well as my thunderbox.' He gave a long, rumbling cough accompanied by a maelstrom of phlegm, then blew his dangling moustache up from his lip, an action that sent ripples through the proliferant side-whiskers as well. 'You'll attend on me, Smyth, as usual.'

'Of course, sir' Captain Smyth, the ADC, tall, thin and very smart, got to his feet and hovered until he was despatched to gather the General's various accessories. Some ten minutes later a small procession, which included the General's bugler who invariably attended upon him for the passing of orders, left the train heavily laden and splashed through the flood-water towards the rising ground. Here the thunderbox, discreetly tented, was set up and General Farrar-Drumm disappeared into the tent and sat ruminantly for about five minutes, with Captain Smyth and the bugler attending upon him from without. At the end of the five minutes there was a shrill whistle from the railway engine and, amid much steam, the train got under way.

Captain Smyth jerked urgently at the tent-flap.

'What was that noise, Smyth?' the General asked.

'The train, sir! It's moving out, sir—'

'Where, for God's sake?'

'Backwards, sir—'

'Tell it to stop, Smyth.'

'Yes, sir.' Captain Smyth ran to the top of the rise, cupped his hands about his mouth and shouted towards the train. 'I say! I say, there! Stop instantly ... oh, damn.' He seized the whistle from the lanyard about his neck, and blew many blasts as the train began to move out of hearing. He waved his arms and danced upon the rising ground, but all to no avail. Even the bugler, blowing a desperate blast on his instrument, remained unregarded.

Smyth reported to his General. 'I'm afraid the train's gone, sir.'

'It'll be back. My Chief of Staff will deal with the blasted engine-driver shortly, I presume.'

'I don't know, sir—'

'What d'yer mean, don't know!'

'There's no communication with the engine, sir. I'm afraid it means waiting until the train reaches the next station, sir.'

'Blasted incompetence! Why the devil did the damn driver leave without me, Smyth? I must have been plain enough to be seen, surely?'

'Not actually, sir. We are on the far side of the hill. The driver may have assumed you'd gone back to the train, sir.'

Farrar-Drumm fumed. 'He ought to be blasted well shot. Damn chi-chis!' he added, in reference to the fact that the railways in India were run almost exclusively by the Anglo-Indians, the half-castes beloved of nobody. If in fact he had been in a position to have the man shot, no one would be worried. In the meantime he was faced with either a long wait or a long march and he liked neither prospect very much. 'Where's the next blasted station, Smyth?' he demanded.

Smyth said, 'I believe it's Patna, sir.'

All the men, the Scots picquets included, had been ordered back aboard the train and the soldiers had taken up their posts at the windows, keeping as far in cover as was possible. As the Pathans advanced across the open space towards the station buildings, Ogilvie passed the word for the men to fire independently; as the bullets began smashing into the native hordes Ogilvie found his arm clutched by Mr Wilberforce of Public Works.

'Captain Ogilvie, we have coal now! Why not start the engine, and move away?'

'Two reasons, Mr Wilberforce: to raise steam will take time even if we have water enough—'

'Water enough, my dear fellow!'

'Yes,' Ogilvie said patiently, 'there's plenty around but possibly not in the tanks. The second reason, and the conclusive one, Mr Wilberforce, is that the track has been washed away both to the east and the west, and—'

'Yes, yes, I'm sorry. I'd failed to take account of that.' Wilberforce pulled down his jacket and seemed to be trying to look martial. 'What d'you rate our chances, Captain Ogilvie?'

'We'll give a good account of ourselves.'

'That fails to answer my question, and as the senior Civilian I am in charge of the train, you realise that, I've no doubt.'

'As a matter of fact, I didn't,' Ogilvie answered coolly. 'In the circumstances, the military take precedence, Mr Wilberforce, and you'll kindly take orders from me, as representing General Fettleworth who sent me here. I suggest you find a rifle and join in the defence.' He turned away, moving along the coach as bullets from the *jezails* spattered the train's sides from both directions. Women and children, white-faced, some of them crying, crouched below the windows in the lee of the seats as the battle continued. Everywhere glass was shattered, the fragments as the bullets struck causing a number of cuts some of which would be serious enough to need first-aid attention and bandages torn from handkerchiefs and shirts. The natives were crouched in the water or behind half-drowned bushes and scrubby trees, and it was clearly going to be a lengthy business before they were driven back and away with their casualties. There was a sense of determination, and a disregard of the British fire. A hundred thousand pounds in gold was an attractive enough objective – attractive enough, evidently, to bring the Pathans all the way from the North-West Frontier! That was a long haul otherwise than by the train; the word about the gold bullion must have leaked, together with its route, quite a long while ago. The floods had simply played, fortuitously, into the Pathans' hands. Ogilvie ducked smartly as a bullet smacked into a seat-back alongside him, splintering the wood. As he moved on a lull came in the firing; and he saw Colour-Sergeant MacTrease splashing at the double along by the track on the safe side of the train carrying his rifle. MacTrease jumped aboard Ogilvie's coach; Ogilvie asked him how things were going in the rear of the train.

'Not too badly, sir,' MacTrease answered, sounding breathless. 'No serious casualties so far, and we've picked off a number of the Pathans, sir.'

'The Maxim—'

'Where you ordered it set up, sir, in the guard's van.'

'Yes. But we may need to use it elsewhere before the gold bullion's directly attacked.'

'Where from, sir?'

'I don't know yet, but I take your point – not many places where it can be used to full effect ... except from the roof of the train.'

'Tricky, sir. Easy enough to pick off the crew, sir.'

'Yes, I realise that, Colour. Anyway, we'll leave it where it is for the time being.'

'Very good, sir.' MacTrease was about to move on when suddenly he stiffened and said, 'The buggers are coming in again, sir.' With Ogilvie, he dropped to his knees and thrust his rifle through a shattered window, and fired fast and blind into an onrush of native bodies. All the Scots rifles were firing and the barrels were growing hot; Pathans seemed to go down like ninepins, clutching chests and throats or flinging up their arms as they fell. Then, as the main flank forces swept on for the train, disregarding their casualties, two small parties, one to the right and the other to the left, were seen to detach in the direction of the guard's van, clearly making straight for the bullion while the main bodies engaged the Scots' defence. Ogilvie shouted orders over the din to MacTrease: 'Two sections, Colour, to close towards the guard's van – one right, one left!'

'Aye, sir.' MacTrease moved off, calling his orders to the section sergeants to deploy onto the track. As he did so, the stutter of the Maxim was heard above the fire from the rifles and jezails, a heartening sound. Ogilvie jumped down to the track and ran for the guard's van: exposing himself foolishly as it turned out. As he doubled along, bent low, a big Pathan, cutting through the Scots' ranks, came straight for him with his *jezail* lifted. Ogilvie aimed his revolver and fired point blank; both men fired in the same split-second. As the Pathan crashed heavily, a bullet from the *jezail* snicked across Ogilvie's skull, knocking him cold. As he fell and lay half beneath the train, the Maxim suddenly went out of action and then a series of explosions was heard from the rear of the train. There was a sheet of flame as the guard's van burst open, flame and smoke through which a number of Pathans could be seen amongst the van's wreckage. Seeing them, Cunningham went along at the rush but was too late: the remainder of the native mass came in howling and shooting to engage the Scots and hold them off. Pinned down and in mortal danger now, the RSM watched helplessly while the looters snatched up the bullion boxes and made off towards the west.

'Grenades, sir,' Cunningham reported. A lance-corporal had spotted Ogilvie as he fell, and had dragged him away and into one of the coaches. 'A devil of a lot of them. The Maxim's crew had no chance at all, Captain Ogilvie.'

Ogilvie nodded, and at once regretted the movement: his head was splitting and blood showed through the rough bandage, put in place by Fiona Elliott. He felt sick and groggy; waves of giddiness swept over him as he tried to stand up. Knowing what the answer must be, he asked, 'The gold, Sar'nt-Major?'

'Gone, sir. All gone – every box. And with it the bloody Pathans. All of them – those that aren't lying dead, that is.'

'All? Not just the ones who attacked the van?'

'All, Captain Ogilvie. There's been some bloody fighting – the Jocks gave as good as they got, but the buggers largely got away on their horses. There's been no further attack, and I don't believe they'll come again. It was the gold they wanted, and the gold they've got. They're not concerned about the train or passengers any more.' Cunningham straightened his Sam Browne belt. 'So what do we do now, Captain Ogilvie?'

'Give me a little time, Sar'nt-Major,' Ogilvie said.

'Yes, sir, of course. I'm sorry to bother you till you're feeling fit. The buggers are in any case well away by now and the chances are—' The Regimental Sergeant-Major broke off, then said in a loud hiss, 'That Mr Wilberforce, sir, is approaching. Shall I have him turned about?'

'No. I'd better hear what he has to say, though I can have a damn good guess it won't be anything congratulatory.' Still giddy, Ogilvie reeled back against the side of the coach, then straightened as the Civilian came up. He said, 'I'm very sorry, Mr Wilberforce—'

'The gold, Captain Ogilvie, the gold! It's gone – gone, do you hear me—'

'I know—'

'One hundred thousand pounds' worth and I responsible for it!'

'Oh, I doubt if—'

'Me personally, as the senior Civilian!'

Wilberforce almost wrung his hands; he was not far off tears by the look of him. 'It's really dreadful, a most terrible calamity! It must be got back, do you hear me – it must be got back!'

'We'll do our best,' Ogilvie said shortly, 'but I can't hold out much hope. I know the tribesmen. For one thing, it'll not stay together long but will be split up until it's safely across the Frontier into Afghanistan. I—'

'You must do something! You must mount an expedition, send your men out—'

Ogilvie cut in, 'I've said already, we shall do our best. I've nothing to add to that, Mr Wilberforce.'

In Ogilvie's view no amount of gold bullion was worth the life of a single one of his Scots, but it was not only the gold *per se* that had to be considered. It was what the Pathans could do with it: buy arms for use against the Raj. There was thus a distinct threat to the stability of British India, or at any rate to the North-West Frontier provinces. There was also the question of the cocked snook: the Raj had to get the gold back or stand discredited in native eyes. Losing no more time once he felt fit, Ogilvie passed the orders to march out to the west, leaving behind a train escort of a corporal and six men who would stand guard over the passengers under the command of the Regimental Sergeant-Major; and leaving orders that the train was to remain in the station rather than be pushed back to where it had been standing earlier. Cunningham was not pleased to be missing the pursuit, but acknowledged that someone of age as well as authority was needed to deal with Civilians and more importantly their women and children: a subaltern could be somewhat out of his depth with domestic problems and would be better employed on the march.

Detailing two men to form the first watch, Cunningham, who would take turn and turn about with Corporal Cameron as guard commander, looked out after the departing Scots. He wished them luck, but was in truth expectant of little success. When needs be, the Pathans could move fast, very fast, and anything short of a cavalry pursuit would stand little chance of overtaking them – they would have more horses held in readiness somewhere nearby. And even a full company would be small beer compared with the support the Pathans could count on along the way into distant Afghanistan. Much luck and much courage were going to be called for. As the hours passed, Cunningham grew more and more morose and dealt shortly with the loudly uttered moans of Mr Wilberforce and a number of his like-minded colleagues. Mr Wilberforce was a very loud-mouthed gentleman indeed in Cunningham's view; a detestable person, not to put too fine a point upon it. As night came down, Cunningham did as he had always done when in the field, which was to make a personal and conscientious patrol of the perimeter of the camp – or in this case, of the train and the station and its environs, just to be on the safe side and spot anything that might look suspicious and possibly indicative of an attack by ordinary bandits, which was not to be ruled out.

Half way around his self-appointed patrol, the Regimental Sergeant-Major did find something suspicious. A person, he was sure, was approaching the station from a south-westerly direction. Not just one person: several persons, some of them – Cunningham saw as they came nearer – carrying something heavy. These persons came in verbal silence, but not in much secrecy. They were advancing quite openly and there was very heavy breathing from at least one of them.

Cunningham, standing stock still, drew out his revolver and aimed it towards the shadowy, night-enshrouded persons. He called out loudly: 'Halt!'

There was a pause, then the reply came: '*What?* What the devil!'

'Who goes there?' Cunningham shouted.

There was an angry sound from the darkness and something thumped on the ground. 'Who the devil are yer?' an autocratic voice, a very English voice, demanded.

Cunningham said, 'I am the Regimental Sergeant-Major of the 114th Highlanders. If you do not identify yourself, it will be my duty to fire upon you.' And he added, taking into account thc voice, 'Sir!'

There was a pause. Then the voice said angrily, 'What damned impudence! A Regimental Sergeant-Major ... no. Captain Smyth, I shall *not* answer friend.' The voice was raised again. 'I am Major-General Sir Clarence Farrar-Drumm, commanding Southern Army, and if there's to be any more damn nonsense I shall have yer blasted well shot.'

Stolidly, Cunningham gave the formal response: 'Advance, friend, and be recognised.'

Six

Sir Clarence Farrar-Drumm cleared his throat noisiliy: his phlegm was bad. 'Walked,' he said briefly in answer to Cunningham's astounded question. 'Damn train went off without me, doncher know. Didn't come back, what's more – don't know what happened but I shall find out, damned if I don't! Where's my ADC?'

'Here, sir.'

'Ah, yes. See to my tent and thunderbox, Smyth.' The General poked his walking-stick towards Cunningham. 'What did yer say yer name was?'

'Cunningham, sir. 114th Highlanders.'

'Kilted?'

'Yes, sir,' Cunningham answered, sounding surprised.

'Can't see in the dark, I'm not a damn cat. Scottish troops ... yes, well. Not too bad, I suppose, but the Scots don't go in for cavalry much, do they, and I'm a cavalryman. Fourth dragoons in my regimental days.' Farrar-Drumm coughed at some length.

'Where are yer billeted, Sar'nt-Major?'
'Aboard the train, sir.'
'Not another damn train? Or is it my train?'
'No, sir.' Cunningham explained the position, pointing towards the bulk of the darkened coaches behind him: he had a feeling that the General's eyesight was not as good as it had once been. 'We're awaiting relief from Patna, sir. Also a repair gang.'
'Patna. That's where I'm supposed to be.'
'Indeed, sir.'
'Where's my blasted ADC?'
'Here, sir.'
'Ah, yes. Find out what happened to my damn train, Smyth. Now, Sar'nt-Major, lead me to this train of yours and I shall assume command.'
'Very good, sir.' As Farrar-Drumm, taking a pace forward, stumbled a little. Cunningham reached out a steadying arm, but this was roughly cast aside.
The General said in a hoarse voice, 'I don't need coddling. I'm as fit as a fiddle, not a blasted invalid in need of a damn nurse.'

'Needle in a haystack, James,' Harrington said next morning, shading his eyes to look ahead at blank, empty barrenness. During the night the Scots had bivouacked under the care of picquets, and under the cold lash of the rain as well. It had been an uncomfortable night, and the drenched men had climbed out from under their so-called waterproof sheeting into a dreary dawn to shave and take a makeshift breakfast and then resume the westward march. Henry Harrington, senior subaltern, squelched with every footstep. 'We've not the ghost of a chance of catching up with the Pathans!'

'We have to try,' Ogilvie said shortly. 'We can pick up a lead, surely!'

Harrington snorted. 'I take leave to differ.'

'Your privilege, my dear chap!' Ogilvie marched doggedly on, knowing that there was much truth in what Harrington had said. Perhaps this was all something of a wild goose chase. Ogilvie's plan, so far as he could have one at all, was to march into the town of Chapra, some twenty miles west of Bundarbar, the principal town of the Saran district of Bengal, where he would make contact with a telegraph line and alert the depleted frontier garrison at Nowshera, who would then presumably send out patrols to watch the routes through into the Afghan hills and scour the intervening country so far as possible. They, too, would face a needle in a haystack, but would have the advantage of operating in their own well-known territory and of the virtually certain knowledge that the gold-bearing Pathans were bound to pass through that territory on the reasonable assumption that they intended to enter Afghanistan. The Nowshera command would, as a matter of routine, alert all units covering Waziristan to the south of the Khyber Pass and the lands to the north leading up to the Hindu Kush. That done. Ogilvie intended to resume the westward march and employ his company to act as it were as beaters, flushing the Pathans before them. It might work out, and it might not. His chief hope was that whilst in Chapra he might manage to pick up some clues; perhaps it was a long shot to be using as a chief hope, but India was, as ever, India. Ears were long and so were the arms astretch for rewards in respect of treachery; and the British Raj used many means towards its ends.

Ogilvie, rubbing the tiredness from his eyes, yawned as he marched in the lead of his company. The land was open enough, and his advance could be seen for many miles in spite of the rain. It was impossible to advance in anonymity. Ogilvie turned to look back at his Scots, clumping along behind with wet uniforms and dour faces. They needed more spring in their step. Ogilvie called for Colour-Sergeant MacTrease, who doubled up smartly from the rear, overtaking the files, and gave Ogilvie a butt salute upon his rifle.

'Sir!'

'The men look as though they're going to a funeral, Colour.'

'I'll smarten them up, sir.'

'No, I'm not criticising! Just let's have the pipes and drums, Colour.'

'Very good, sir.' MacTrease saluted again, then turned about and called for the two pipers and the drummers. The men doubled ahead of the advance and took up their position. Air was blown into the bags, the drums beat out the step, and soon the march was enlivened by the tune of 'We're No' Awa''. The men took it up in strong voice, and the words rolled out across the damp, dreary Indian plain:

> 'We're no' awa' tae bide awa'
> We're no' awa' tae leave ye;
> We're no' awa' tae bide awa'
> We'll aye come back and see ye.
> As I gae'd doon by Wilson toon
> I met auld Johnny Scobie;
> Says I tae him, will ye hae a hauf,
> Says he, man, that's ma hobby.
> So we had a hauf, and another hauf,
> And then we had another;
> When he got fu', he shouted, Hoo!
> It's Cam Loch Mill for ever...'

'Burning?' Farrar-Drumm's heavy white eyebrows rose in astonishment at what Mr Wilberforce was telling him. 'Isn't that what the blasted Parsees do with their dead – burn 'em?'

Wilberforce shook his head. 'No, no, General, you're thinking of the towers of silence – the Parsees place their dead on gratings at the top, and the vultures pick the bones clean and then—'

'Yes, yes, all right, I take yer point, the Parsees don't burn. Who does?'

'The Hindus, General—'

'Ah yes, the burning ghats. Calcutta ... yes, you're quite right, Wilberforce, though I don't see that it makes a ha'porth of difference, they're all heathens. However, the British don't burn.'

'Exactly. The whole thought is abhorrent.'

'Who's idea was it, did yer say?'

'Captain Ogilvie's.'

'Ah.'

Wilberforce sniffed. 'The military mind ... I'm sorry, General.' He looked confused. 'I had no intention of – er—'

'Sounding impertinent.'

'Yes. I do apologise, most sincerely. General.'

'Glad yer do. In my view, the miltary mind's a damn sight better than the civilian one.' Farrar-Drumm wheezed and his chest rumbled as he tried to clear his throat. He had a suspicion that he had been sitting in a draught, and draughts were ominous things. Damn the train, and damn Wilberforce too who had sat him in the blasted draught. 'Why did Captain Ogilvie reach this decision to burn the dead, pray?'

'Disease, General.'

'Disease, eh? Disease!' Sir Clarence Farrar-Drumm had seen much disease in his time, in the Crimea, in Zululand, in Bechuanaland, Aden, and here in India; and he had not liked what he had seen. Blackwater fever, malaria, cholera, typhus, dysentery ... men turned black and green, grew distended, bloated, it was horrible. And nothing spread with the lightning rapidity of disease. And that draught – it had already weakened him. Farrar-Drumm pulled anxiously at his white moustache, and thus drew down the heavy bags beneath his eyes. Goodness gracious! He was not an old man, God preserve him from the very thought, but in all honesty neither was he a young one.

'I dislike disease, Wilberforce,' he said. 'Ogilvie was right. They'll have to burn. Didn't yer say, some had been burned already?'

'Yes. That man Cunningham saw to it yesterday. But there are so many—'

'Still waiting, yes.'

'And fires were drawn at nightfall, so as not to make the train stand out—'

'Quite right. I shall start the fires again now.'

'I don't like it, General.'

'You'll have to damn well lump it, then.'

'I shall protest,' Wilberforce said huffily, 'the moment I reach Calcutta. I consider your attitude high-handed in the extreme. When I reach Calcutta—'

'*If* you reach Calcutta!' Farrar-Drumm snapped, his colour almost scarlet, partly from a sudden bout of coughing. 'If you argue with me any more I'll have you damn well shot and then you'll burn with the others!' He raised his voice for the Regimental Sergeant-Major, and passed the orders. As on the day before, the fire was lit beneath the boiler of the engine and while the coal began to glow red the remaining corpses were placed in a precise line on the station platform alongside the coaches. Farrar-Drumm himself, in the absence of a chaplain, read a simple committal service over them all collectively; and read it with dignity and reverence. Then, one by one, the sad remains were lifted by the Scots and carried slowly to the engine, where they were brought aboard and fed through the furnace door to be cleanly consumed. Smell arose, to be wafted back over the silent coaches, held down by the continuing rain so that the ordeal was a long one. As the dreadful process continued, General Farrar-Drumm, aided by his walking-stick and attended by Captain Smyth, moved along the coaches having a word with the bereaved families, assuring them that England and Her Majesty would be proud of the sacrifice...

'Made,' Fiona Elliott said as the General moved past her, 'in the name of gold. In the name of money.'

Farrar-Drumm stopped, eyebrows lifted. 'I beg your pardon, young lady?'

Fiona repeated what she had said, firmly.

'What balderdash!' Farrar-Drumm said in astonished indignation. 'England – not money. I won't have that. Who are you?'

'Fiona Elliott. My uncle is the second-in-command of the Royal Strathspey.'

'His name?'

She said, 'Lord Brora.'

'Brora, Brora.' Farrar-Drumm pursed his lips. 'Gad! I remember the man! Awful ass, quite impossible. Rude and arrogant, dreadful fellow. Well-connected, of course – that's something these days when we're getting so many common officers. I remember him when I was last in the north, ridding the place of that blasted feller who called himself the Star of Islam...' He paused. 'Did yer say yer were his niece?' he asked, sounding very slightly disconcerted.

Fiona was smiling broadly. 'Yes, I did, General, and please don't apologise. I agree with every word you've just said.'

'Really, really! Well, in that case I won't,

only it's a funny world and getting funnier. No damn loyalty left and more's the pity, even if yer don't like the bu – yer uncle.' Farrar-Drumm wheezed for a moment. 'Tell me something, Miss – er—'

'Elliott.'

'Ah yes, Miss Elliott. Young Ogilvie of yer regiment. I gather he's been here in charge. He's another I remember. A good young feller, isn't he?'

'*I* think so,' Fiona said with a touch of primness, and blushed a little as she said it.

'Ha!' Farrar-Drumm said. A hint of a leer came into his watery blue eyes as he recognised the symptoms. He reached out a veined hand covered with liver spots and put it somewhere round Fiona's back. 'Yer a good-looking gel. Young Ogilvie's a fortunate feller. Wish I could shed ten years or so.' Coughing, he released Fiona and moved on along the train. Then he turned back. 'Meant to ask yer another question. Somebody told me but I forget what. Young Ogilvie where's he gone?'

'Looking for gold,' Fiona said. Her tone was hard but there was a sparkle of tears in her eyes; James Ogilvie could become another life lost to the god of gold bullion. Every minute, he stood in danger.

B Company of the Royal Strathspey entered the town of Chapra behind the pipes and drums. There was nothing to be lost and everything to be gained by entering smartly, martially and with pride as the representatives of the British Raj and its might, the representatives of Her Majesty the Queen-Empress, the distant Mother of her Peoples ruling from the great metropolis of London. Chapra did not often witness the march of one of Her Majesty's British regiments on foot; and the population turned out in their thousands to stare as the pipes and drums went by with a swing of kilt and sporran. Ogilvie knew that the natives of India liked the pipes as much as did the Scots themselves; and he made the most of it. A lance-corporal was detached to seek a native guide to the British Residency; and a man came forward willingly and placed himself in front of the pipes and drums, marching to the step of the company and using his arms policeman-like to indicate the route.

Inside the Residency, Ogilvie was given the freedom of the telegraph. He sent a full report to the acting garrison commander in Nowshera, requesting action and indicating his own intentions. This done, he joined the Resident, Humphrey Pollinger, in a *chota peg*. Pollinger had had certain news through from Patna, where General Fettleworth was bothered about his missing fellow-general, Sir Clarence Farrar-Drumm.

'Poor old Farrar-Drumm got left behind,'

Pollinger said. 'Somewhere south-west of Patna. Perhaps you'd better look out for him as well.'

'I'll be going the other way,' Ogilvie said. Pollinger went on to say that Farrar-Drumm had been looked for but with no success so far. The driver of his train, when questioned, had said he believed the General had returned aboard after using his thunderbox and he hadn't heard the furious shouts from the windows of the leading coach; he had admitted to being almost stone deaf and could only just hear his own engine even on the foot-plate, while his fireman had been too busily engaged in wielding his shovel. It was a sad business, but Farrar-Drumm had his ADC with him plus some *sepoys* of Southern Army; he might yet turn up. If he did not, the loss to the Raj would not be catastrophic.

'If there's any assistance I can give,' Pollinger said, 'you've only to ask. In regard to your march west, I mean.'

Ogilvie nodded his thanks. 'Have you any ears to the ground?' he asked.

'Of course I have, that's my daily bread. But I have to confess there's been absolutely nothing about your gold. Yet, anyway. It may come. If it does, I'll inform Nowshera immediately. My offer of assistance was really in regard to material things – commissariat, for instance.'

'I was going to ask about that,' Ogilvie said. He had felt obliged to leave behind some of his precious food stocks for the use of the passengers aboard the train. 'I have a list of my requirements all ready to hand, as a matter of fact.' He grinned. 'I hope you don't mind the touch of presumption, if that's the word—'

'Good heavens, no, it's your duty and mine too.' Pollinger reached out for the stores indent, read it briefly, and said, 'I'll have all this ready for you within an hour – no trouble at all.'

Ogilvie thanked him again and said he would provide a party with commissariat carts. Refusing the offer of another *chota peg*, Ogilvie rejoined his company outside the Residency, and whilst awaiting the stores passed the time in walking up and down with his subalterns as though he were changing the palace guard in London. Meanwhile the pipers played on to an admiring crowd; and the native guide who had led them in remained as it were on parade with his hands clasped in apparent reverence for the stirring sounds of Scotland. As promised, the commissariat carts arrived back, heavily laden, within the hour. Taking his leave of Pollinger outside the Residency, Ogilvie passed the word to MacTrease to march out of the town to the west.

He caught the eye of the guide. 'You will lead again?' he asked in Urdu.

The man salaamed. 'Of course. Captain sahib. It is my honour and my privilege, Captain sahib.' Once again he placed himself ahead of the pipes and drums; the company marched out to the tune of 'A Hundred Pipers an' A'. More crowds lined the streets as they marched away; and then, as the open country was seen not far ahead, the guide detached himself from the lead and slid back to walk alongside the Captain sahib, who felt in his pockets for a handful of rupees by way of reward.

'Thanks, old chap,' the guide said, grinning.

Ogilvie gasped. 'What the bloody hell—'

'All right, all right, I'm not getting uppish. The name's Harlow. Political Service.' A brown-stained hand came out. 'I'll take the rupees, thanks, in the interest of authenticity and because I have to eat now and again.' He paused, eyeing Ogilvie's still astonished face. 'Can I help? British units usually come for a purpose, if only to beat the drum – and in that case it's announced ahead. My devious mind tells me there's nothing routine about your visit.'

Ogilvie, still marching on, nodded. 'You're right, but...'

'But what? You don't trust me – that's natural and quite proper. I'll try to help.'

Harlow rattled off a good deal of precise detail about the command structure in Nowshera and Peshawar, naming names and ranks. He added, 'Your Divisional Political Officer's Blaise-Willoughby, the man with the monkey. Calls it Wolseley, which is libellous on our good Commander-in-Chief at home. I gather Blaise-Willoughby's in Patna with Bloody Francis.'

'That's right, he is.'

'Well? Can I help?'

'Do you know anything about gold bullion?' Ogilvie asked.

'It weighs a lot. Why?'

'There was a consignment of it – Murree to Calcutta.' Briefly, Ogilvie explained what had happened. Harlow, it seemed, had heard nothing about the movement of the bullion from Murree and, as he said, there was no reason why he should. Such distant matters were not his concern. Likewise, he had picked up no whispers in the bazaars and alleys of Chapra as to the seizure from the train nor of any Pathans riding hot-foot for the Frontier. But from now on he would make it very much his concern to find out more.

'Leave it to me,' he said.

'If you find anything out, how do you make contact?'

'With you?' Harlow gave a quiet laugh. 'Perhaps I won't. I doubt if those Pathans of yours will be lingering in the vicinity, somehow! They'll be well west by now ... anything I find out would be better used in Nowshera, I fancy. On the other hand—'

'On the other hand,' Ogilvie broke in, 'they could be lying doggo, couldn't they, waiting until the watch on the Frontier dies down a little?'

'That's what I was about to say. It's a possibility, no more than that – an outside chance. If I find out anything that tends to that view, I'll get in touch.'

'How?'

Harlow laid his right forcfinger against his nose and winked. 'Leave that to me as well. I shall get word of where you're to be found, don't worry!'

And that was all: Harlow moved away, doubling a little ahead of the pipes and drums, then stood aside with his right hand raised in a native version of the British military salute as the Scots marched by. As the rear files went past the Political Officer turned back into the town, once more a low-caste native who had been of some brief service to the soldiers of the Raj. Ogilvie's feeling was that Harlow had been somewhat indiscreet in his obvious fawning upon British uniforms. Such could hardly help his charade amongst the kind of native element from whom he might be hoping for whispers about British gold.

* * *

'Sar'nt-Major!'

Cunningham, marching down the track, turned as he heard his name called from the train. General Farrar-Drumm was thrusting his white-haired head from a window, looking agitated. Cunningham turned about, marched back, and slammed to the salute.

'Sir!'

'Sar'nt-Major, I dislike inactivity. The limbs tend to stiffen up, doncher know.'

'Yes, sir.'

'It's not just that, however.' Farrar-Drumm cleared his throat. 'No damn repair gangs yet.'

'No, sir. With respect, sir, the land's still under flood.'

'Yes, I am aware of that, thank you, Sar'nt-Major, but I am not convinced it's entirely relevant. The blasted flood's not as deep now, is it, and I should have thought it possible for repair gangs to damn well wade through so as to be on the spot and ready the moment the waters recede. What?'

'Yes, sir, maybe so.'

Farrar-Drumm went on, 'I tell yer what the trouble is, Sar'nt-Major: General Fettleworth is not aware that I'm here. If he knew that, he'd obviously take action, wouldn't he?'

'Aye, sir, I expect he would. But I don't doubt, sir, that General Fettleworth knows from the reports when your own train reached Patna, that you're somewhere in the vicinity.'

'Ah, yes, but he can't be sure, doncher see. He can't be sure that I'm aboard this train, that's the point as I see it. I intend sending two of my *sepoys* through to Patna to report my whereabouts, but since they're only too likely to get themselves lost, I want one of your men to go with them.'

Cunningham said, 'With respect, sir, I have only just enough men to maintain picquets as it is, and—'

'Oh, bother take the picquets, Sar'nt-Major, I feel quite sure we're not going to come under further attack now the damn bullion's gone. I'd send my ADC only I can't spare him. See to it, if you please, at once.'

The aged head was withdrawn. Cunningham blew angrily through his moustache. Daft old dodderer ... but that was no way to think about the GOC Southern Army! Marching back along the platform and calling for the off-duty picquets, Cunningham reflected dourly that if the *sepoys* from Ootacamund were likely to get lost then so, if not more so, was Captain Smyth, who had a very half-baked look about him. But if there was action, a Scots private was going to be of much more use to the train's defence than Captain Smyth.

* * *

As night came down again and the flickering tallow lamps of Chapra glowed through the darkness, the Political Officer made his clandestine way to the Street of the Silk Sellers. The shops, all of them open, were small and stuffed with their precious wares, either in highly-coloured rolls or spread wide for the customers to see them better. The yellow lamp-light flickered over every colour of the prism and every conceivable combination of those colours: it was a feast for the eye. The street was crowded as Harlow pushed through, making for the shop of one Lal Chatterjee, a youngish trader with many in-laws to support and placate. One of these was currently lording it amid the bales of silk: Lal Chatterjee's mother-in-law, old and immensely fat, and ugly.

The Political Officer bowed his head to the old woman and held his hands, palms together, before his face in the Hindu greeting. In return he received a hard stare.

'What is it you want, Ram Dhavan?'

'Lal Chatterjee, your son-in-law.'

'As usual, my son-in-law does nothing, and does it in the back of the shop,' the harridan answered. 'Go to him, then, and tell him if he does not stir himself, his mother-in-law will die of the work he does not do himself.'

The Political Officer hid a grin and made his way to the back of the premises bearing these glad tidings to Lal Chatterjee, who was in fact engaged upon some book-work for the benefit of the Collector of Taxes for the Bengal Presidency. After the polite formalities Lal Chatterjee asked directly what Ram Dhavan came to him for; and added in a tone of reproof that his visitor had been observed that morning giving assistance to the soldiers of the Raj and cavorting himself as though he enjoyed marching at their head.

'Who brought you this report?'

'One of my uncles-in-law,' Chatterjee answered, dipping his quill into some red ink.

'And did this one of your relatives inform you further that I talked for some while to the Captain sahib, when the soldiers were leaving the town, Lal Chatterjee?'

'He did, Ram Dhavan.'

The Political Officer nodded. 'I thought perhaps so. I spoke much to the Captain sahib, Lal Chatterjee, and with purpose. It was indeed with purpose that I gave my services as guide.'

'And the purpose?' The quill was laid aside now, and keen eyes stared intently through steel-rimmed spectacles set upon a blunt, stub-like nose.

The Political Officer leaned forward and spoke now in a low tone, casting wary glances towards the bead curtain that separated Lal Chatterjee from his mother-in-law. He said, 'The Captain sahib seeks gold.'

The eyes glittered. 'Gold, Ram Dhavan? What gold?'

'British gold. Gold taken from the stranded train at Bundarbar ... the Captain sahib asked many questions. The gold, which is in bullion form, is said to be worth one hundred thousand sterling pounds, Lal Chatterjee.'

A rapid mental sum was done: a rupee was worth one shilling and fourpence sterling. The answer was something over one and a half million rupees. Lal Chatterjee took off his spectacles and wiped them with a trembling hand. One and a half million rupees, if ever he should possess such a sum, would make his mother-in-law eat out of his hand, and there would of course be many other advantages too. Hoarsely Lal Chatterjee asked, 'What is it you are suggesting to me, Ram Dhavan?'

Harlow shrugged. He said, 'The Captain sahib indicated to me that some Pathans had stolen the gold. He asked me if I had seen Pathans in Chapra, and I answered honestly that I had not, nor had I heard talk of them. Tell me, Lal Chatterjee: have *you* heard of such Pathans ... such evil men as to steal gold from the Raj?'

Lal Chatterjee returned his look and his

grin. Many emotions passed across the silk merchant's face, one after the other. Then he said, 'No, Ram Dhavan. I know nothing of any Pathans.'

Harlow looked disappointed, but shrugged. 'You are the eyes and the ears of Chapra,' he said. 'If you have not heard, then there are no Pathans in the town, or near it either.'

'That is true.'

'It is a pity,' the Political Officer said.

'Yes, a pity.' The quill pen was taken up again. 'Now I am a busy man, Ram Dhavan, with many, many hours of work ahead of me.'

'And many, many relatives to support,' Harlow said rather nastily. He took his leave, making his way back into the street past the mother-in-law, who was negotiating the sale of a length of sky-blue silk. He slunk into an alley opposite, from where he could watch the shop of Lal Chatterjee. He knew the silk merchant well, and could read his face like an open book. It had been a very long shot indeed but he believed something had registered. If so, it was down to luck alone; and he was still dubious as to the Pathans having lingered in the vicinity. But, after a very long wait, his patience was rewarded. A furtive-looking Lal Chatterjee, skull-capped and wearing a long, tunic-necked coat of a dark colour, emerged from the shop and, looking everywhere at once but trying not to appear to do so, set off at a brisk pace towards the northern end of the street.

At a discreet distance, the Political Officer followed.

Seven

'Two sepoys and a Scots private?' Fettleworth stared in surprise. 'What the devil do they want with me, Lakenham?'

'They bring a report, sir. An important one.'

Fettleworth ran a hand round the inside of his collar-band: Patna was still damp and sticky and flooded and so far he had been unable to move his division out to the east as previously ordered. 'Well, go on, then, for God's sake!'

The Chief of Staff said, 'General Farrar-Drumm has been found, sir.'

'Damn! Where?'

'In the train at Bundarbar. It seems he's currently unable to reach Patna unless—'

'Thank God.'

Lakenham coughed. 'That may be so, sir, but he asks for repair gangs to be sent to free him—'

'Can't. Land's still flooded,' Fettleworth said promptly. 'Farrar-Drumm will simply have to wait, that's all, and good luck to him!'

'Yes, sir. But that's not all. He's sent a written despatch.' Lakenham produced a small sheet of paper torn from a notebook and covered with spidery writing in pencil, folded in half and sealed with a piece of stamp paper. This he handed over with a flourish. 'General Farrar-Drumm has no doubt reported upon the whole situation of the train, sir.'

'Silly old fool,' Fettleworth muttered angrily He ripped at the stamp paper and began to read without much interest. Then he stiffened and his face lost some of its high colour. He thrust the paper at his Chief of Staff. 'Just look at that, Lakenham! My God! Some buggers have stolen a consignment of gold for Calcutta!' He bounded to his feet; the trestle table that currently represented Division was sent flying as he heaved his stomach up. 'Get repair gangs out immediately Lakenham, and have that damn train brought in!'

'As you said earlier, sir, the land's still flooded—'

'Oh, balls, what does that matter? The damn repair gangs will just have to make the best they can of it and if they fail to get through I'll have them all in the town jail.'

'My dear sir,' Lakenham said tartly, 'railway lines can scarcely be straightened and built up while they're still under water.'

'Yes, they can if I say so. Don't dither,

Lakenham, just get on with it!' Fettleworth marched up and down the room shaking both fists in the air. This was terrible; it approached tragedy and it wasn't fair. It really wasn't his job to guard gold aboard somebody else's damn train, but he knew very well that Calcutta would blame him since Bundarbar could be considered as within his current area of command – and *he* had sent young Ogilvie, who would soon feel the full weight of his displeasure, to do something – he couldn't remember what – about the bloody train! It would all come down to him, as all balls-ups throughout British history had come down to the senior military officer on the spot. His Excellency would be furious, so would the Commander-in-Chief in Calcutta, Sir George White. So – God help him – would Whitehall and Her Majesty! One hundred thousand pounds would buy a vast amount of guns and rifles and explosives to be used against the Raj. He, Fettleworth, would be dishonoured, prematurely retired. And he knew, with a terrible knowledge that seared his soul, what awaited officers prematurely retired from Her Majesty's service: Cheltenham, or Bath.

Lal Chatterjee seemed to be no longer suspicious, feeling himself safe: there were no more backward looks and he was losing no time. Harlow had some difficulty in keeping up with him, but keep up he did as Chatterjee traversed half Chapra. Through one smelly alley after another, almost falling over the outthrust feet of the beggars lying across the route, slipping on the filthy overflows of the open sewers, dodging the teeth of the brutish pariah dogs who normally turned tail and slunk away but didn't when trodden upon inadvertently. Harlow followed his quarry. Some of the alleys were still crowded, and Harlow often had to push his way through and thus incur abuse and the threatening sight of ready knives and daggers and of rusted bayonets purloined from the Raj. Foul smells wafted from the doorways of the hovels to do battle with the drains; from some lamp-lit windows women looked with inviting smiles and gestures; from others came screams and cries as God knew what took place within. Chapra at night – any city of the Indian subcontinent at night – was not a pleasant or healthy place to be.

And Chatterjee was going on and on, and on again. The journey seemed endless.

At last the end did come.

It came in a hovel on the very outskirts of the town, almost the last human dwelling in Chapra. Lal Chatterjee halted; so did the Political Officer, who flattened into a doorway. He heard the bang of a fist on wood farther along, and when he peered out from his doorway, Lal Chatterjee had vanished. The Political Officer lost no time in taking a risk: not very large a risk, for India was India and the homeless beggars were legion. The Political Officer would be merely one more. Moving along the street, he huddled himself into the ground below the window of a room in the hovel just entered by Lal Chatterjee. Then he listened; but he was out of luck. No voices came, and no light appeared in the room. The Political Officer got to his feet again, and moved on in the direction of the open countryside, but before reaching it turned around the angle of the last of the dwellings and made towards the back of the hovel where Lal Chatterjee was closeted.

At the back was a light; the Political Officer approached the window, moving cautiously. Rough sacking was draped across, but there was a gap at the top. Standing on tiptoe, the Political Officer had a reasonable view of the room. And there was Lal Chatterjee, talking earnestly to a fellow Hindu, a gross man whose features had been badly scarred by the smallpox and one of whose ears was missing: the ear was represented by no more than a small curl of flesh. Lal Chatterjee was excited, and had communicated his excitement to the gross man: voices came through, albeit in snatches: enough, at any rate, for the

Political Officer to get the gist of the conversation. He gathered that the gross man was a moneychanger and lender, also a dealer in stolen goods. Had word reached him of gold bars purloined from the Raj? At first, it had not; but Lal Chatterjee was familiar enough with his own kind, and he persisted. It was early days yet, but soon the great Raj would be sure to offer a reward for information leading to the recovery of the gold. This reward would be substantial, a forecast in which the gross man appeared to concur. The reward, Lal Chatterjee said, could well be equally shared, a suggestion with which the gross man was not in agreement. That would be such a pity, Lal Chatterjee remarked, for he had no wish in the world to be forced to make life difficult for such a man as the gross one, who stood largely beyond the law in his trading.

The gross man took the point, but made another in return: the seeking of information was to be left to him alone and if and when he found it, then he would at once make contact with Lal Chatterjee and a fair division could be worked out. To this, Lal Chatterjee was obliged to agree; but urged speed since a force of British soldiers was already in pursuit of the Pathans and might recover the gold in the meantime. This speed the gross man promised most faithfully. Outside, the Political Officer grinned to himself: there would be little honour among thieves and it was patently obvious that neither Lal Chatterjee nor the gross man had any intention of bothering about pittances of rewards but would aim for the main chance if at all possible – the gold itself. As the talking went on, the Political Officer formed the impression that the gross man knew a good deal more about the theft than he had let on to Lal Chatterjee; and he formed a suspicion that the gold might well have been hidden away in Chapra by the Pathans pending transportation into Afghanistan at a more propitious moment. Or, alternatively, that a determined band of Hindus led by the gross man himself might decide to overtake the Pathans and seize the booty for themselves ... in the meantime, the conversation continued a while longer; it was not so loud now, less intense since the bargaining was over, but the Political Officer heard just enough to realise that Lal Chatterjee was being pumped for any unshed information he might have as to the movement of the British gold-retrieval force, and any other relevant matters. He had none; and rose in due course to take his leave of the gross man. The Political Officer, about to make himself very scarce, was lowering himself from his tiptoe position at the window when the half-expected happened.

Lal Chatterjee turned his back upon the gross man in order to leave the room and the gross man acted very fast: a long knife came out from beneath his clothing and was plunged deep into Lal Chatterjee's ample back. The Political Officer heard no sound at all other than a crash when the body hit a table, but his eyes told him that the silk merchant was very dead indeed.

B Company was well away by now from the flooded areas but Ogilvie could find no tracks, no spoor of any kind. The Pathans had vanished, if ever they had come this way at all. Colour-Sergeant MacTrease, after they had passed through a tiny village where every man had been questioned without any success, became sardonic.

'It's good exercise for the Jocks, sir, and that's about the extent of it,' he said gloomily.

'We'll pick up something soon, Colour.'

'Aye, sore feet! The land's too vast, sir, to my way o' thinking.'

'Nonsense, Colour. We've done it before ... something similar, anyway, in more difficult territory at that. The hills and the passes are a very different kettle of fish from open country.'

'Aye, that's very true, sir.' MacTrease eased the straps of his field equipment. 'That's why I believe they're nowhere around. The Pathans, sir. If they were, we'd be able to see the buggers ten miles off! And they'd be bound to leave tracks behind them, they just couldn't help doing so, sir.'

MacTrease was right; the needle-in-a-haystack element was very strong now. Ogilvie passed the word to halt the company and fall out for a rest and a smoke. He searched the terrain all around through his field glasses: it was flat, dead flat and ugly as far as the eye could see, with just a hint of low hills to the north. Those hills were perhaps twenty miles away, and if the Pathans were there any British advance would be seen very well ahead of its arrival. And surely the Pathans wouldn't be there; if they had got so far, they wouldn't linger but would ride on, increasing the distance between themselves and the pursuit and then evade the patrols from Nowshera and slip anonymously across the Frontier, using one of the countless passes that were well known to the Afghan tribesmen but in many cases, even now, unknown to the British.

Ogilvie paced up and down, deep in thought, smoking a pipe. After a while he called his subalterns together and put his thoughts into words. 'The patrols from Nowshera are going to have the usual sticky time,' he said, 'but in all conscience they'll have a better chance than us! At least they know the likely areas of convergence.

Agree?'

Harrington lifted his eyebrows at his junior, a second lieutenant, then nodded at Ogilvie. 'Agree, James. Are you proposing we march back to Bundarbar?'

'That's right,' Ogilvie answered. 'I suppose it's a kind of retreat, but—'

'Oh, rot!' Harrington said, and laughed. 'It's no retreat, James, it's common sense. We've been wasting our time, that's all.'

'You mean you think I was wrong to march?'

'I rather think so, James, old boy, but never fear, even Bloody Francis has been known to change his mind!'

Ogilvie grinned and called up MacTrease. He passed the orders for the company to fall in for the march back to Bundarbar and the train, which might or might not be there still – would be, Ogilvie fancied; it would take time to repair the line to Patna even after the floods subsided. Now that he was marching back, he was consumed with impatience to get there quickly. Anything could have happened and Fiona was at risk with the others. He could have been guilty of dereliction of duty in leaving the train virtually undefended, but, as ever, it was an officer's choice, an officer's decision between two conflicting duties, and afterwards those in authority were free to apportion praise or blame according to the fortunes of war – success, or failure. But if anything should happen to Fiona he would never forgive himself. So the march back was made at forced pace and the brief halts were the minimum essential to rest the men. As the sun went down the sky that evening they were back in the village through which they had passed going the other way; and the population had turned out to watch them march through.

'Give them a free show, sir?' MacTrease suggested. 'The pipes and drums?'

'Carry on, Colour.'

The pipes and drums struck up as the company came to the start of the village, and the Jocks marched with heads high and chests out to the tune of 'The Barren Rocks of Aden'. As they came into the centre of the village there was a disturbance: a man ran forward to approach Ogilvie – a native, who was at once seized by the villagers and dragged away, but not before Ogilvie had recognised him: Harlow, the Political Officer from Patna. Ogilvie shouted for the pipes and drums to stop their playing and for the company to stand to and fix bayonets. Then, with MacTrease at his side, he ran towards the group of struggling natives.

'Release that man!' he shouted.

There were derisive yells, and gesticulations. Fists were shaken towards the British. Ogilvie repeated his order. 'If you don't do as I say by the time I've counted to ten, I shall open fire and then burn down the village.'

There was a tense silence. Everyone seemed to be holding his breath. The officer sahib's words had rung true, and it would not be the first time that the Raj had burned down a village, though usually this was done only as a reprisal after some act of bloodshed. The silence was broken by a shout in English from the Political Officer.

'Ogilvie, a man to the west – running out of the village. *Get him!*'

Ogilvie turned in a flash, saw the running man, and called the order to the rear files of his soldiers. Two rifles opened and the man crashed, and the rifles of the rest of the company swung to both sides on Harrington's command to cover the villagers. There was another silence while the man on the ground thrashed and moaned. Then the Political Officer was released, and walked towards Ogilvie. 'Just in time,' he said. 'Many thanks!'

'Don't mention it! I think you'd better explain just as soon as you can. We have a nasty situation on our hands by the look of it.'

Eight

The situation was brittle, but the natives were being circumspect. There were too many rifles around, and they didn't like the cold steel threat of the bayonets. Harlow said, 'The first thing I suggest is that you surround the village. It's not large, as you can see. I don't want anyone to get out.'

'Why?'

'Because they'll warn the Pathans. Talking of which, it's a thundering pity you came in with your pipes and drums. But more of that anon. Just get the place surrounded, will you?'

Harlow sounded urgent. Ogilvie passed the orders and the men deployed, spreading out to MacTrease's direction to hem the village and its occupants in. Ogilvie walked down to look at the man who had been shot: he was now dead, shot through the back of the chest and stomach, and there was a spreading pool of blood that reflected back the last rays of the declining sun. The situation was nasty in the extreme; Ogilvie had the feeling that at any moment the villagers might break out and chance the British bullets, that at any time from now on he and his men would be liable to the sudden thrust of a knife in the back. He turned on the Political Officer.

'Let's have it!' he said in a harsh tone. 'I imagine you've lost your usefulness to the Political Service now, haven't you?'

'Yes, but only locally, and new disguises aren't hard to find. Nor are some other things!'

'What d'you mean?'

Harlow grinned. 'Your Pathans.'

'You know where they are?'

'Near enough, yes. I'll try to put it in a nutshell.' As briefly as possible, the Political Officer told Ogilvie about Lal Chatterjee and his night journey, and the silk merchant's subsequent murder by the gross man with the smallpox-scarred face. Hard on the heels of the killing, Harlow had crashed in with his British Army pattern revolver drawn, taking a chance, which paid off, that the gross Hindu was alone in his house. The moneychanger had been scared stiff when Harlow had told him he had witnessed the murder and intended to haul the killer before the British Resident immediately, en route for the town jail and the gallows. Only one thing could save him, and that was to come clean as to his knowledge of the gold bullion. The Hindu, who loved life well enough, had lost no time at all in talking most eloquently. Hindu or not, he had had contact with the Pathans, who of course were Muslims, but there were times – and this, considering the size of the haul, was one of them – when other considerations came before any man's religion. The moneychanger, by name Lakshni Patel, was well-known for his financial accommodations, noted indeed throughout India both north and south. And, being a wealthy man, also one of many established markets, he was negotiating to buy the gold from the Pathans.

'The Pathans see this as a safer bet,' Harlow explained. 'It's easier to slip back into Afghanistan with cash than with gold.'

'Do I gather the transaction's not yet been made?'

Harlow nodded. 'That's right. The Pathans still have the gold, and Patel is currently arranging to assemble the hard cash—'

'Is? Not was?'

'Is.' Harlow gave a sly grin. 'I've gone in with him, for a cut. He's still at large, and will be until the net draws tight!'

'And the Pathans?'

'They're in hiding, probably in the hills to the north, not far from here – Patel wouldn't tell me exactly where, he fears a double-cross I think and he's perfectly right to do so. But it's not important. This is: I know where the exchange is to be made, with proper safeguards for both sides. Patel has another quite reasonable fear, and this is, that when the Pathans have got the cash, they'll kill him and then they'll have the cash as well as the gold. So proper security arrangements have been made.'

'You know the timing as well?'

'Yes, certainly. The deed's to be done here, in this village, after full dark tomorrow. One hundred thousand pounds' worth of gold bullion will meet ninety thousand pounds' worth of Patel's excellent rupees, and then two sets of rascals ride away with their spoils at the expense of the Raj. It's really all very simple.' Harlow went on to explain that after extracting the information from the moneychanger he had come out to the village to reconnoitre the land in advance and had fallen foul of the villagers simply because he was from other parts and thus, at a time of danger, an object of suspicion. 'The village is in on this, you see,' he went on. 'They had to be. They're going to form Patel's protection against getting murdered. They're getting a cut, too.'

'I thought you said it was simple!'

'It was, until you turned up in glory, my dear chap. Now all parties will have to think again. No one's going to make any hand-overs with British troops cordoning the village.'

'That was your idea—'

'I know, I know. It was essential to stop any of the villagers taking word about me to the Pathans, once I'd been seen to be a British agent. That's still essential ... and the rest has yet to be worked out afresh.' Harlow lifted his hands, palms uppermost. 'At this moment, I haven't an idea in my head. Have you?'

Ogilvie shook his head. 'No. But just as a matter of academic interest, how would you have coped if I hadn't turned up? I mean, you could scarcely have arrested Patel and the Pathans on your own, could you?'

'Of course not, and I didn't intend to. The Pathans would have been allowed to go scot free as a matter of fact. I would have arrested Patel with the gold as soon as we got back to Chapra, the Raj would have been happy, and Patel would have been chucked into the jail charged with killing Lal Chatterjee and trying to do a deal against the Raj, which would have bloody well served him right!'

'And the Pathans? They just go right ahead and use the rupees to buy arms? They might just as well be left with the gold, mightn't they?'

Harlow chuckled. 'Oh, no! All those rupees, or most of them anyway, would be forgeries. And arms dealers always make a very special point of ensuring that they don't get fobbed off with forgeries, let me tell you!'

'Perhaps,' Ogilvie said. 'But you can't let the Pathans get away with plunder and murder. What about the killings, back in Bundarbar?'

'Pathans are Pathans,' the Political Officer said with a shrug. 'They all steal and they all kill. We can't arrest and exterminate them all, so why worry about one bunch getting away, so long as the gold's recovered at no expense to the Raj?'

Ogilvie's mouth hardened. 'I've lost men from my company. To me, that's expense enough!'

'Yes, I'm sorry about that, of course—'

'There's a difference of outlook, isn't there? Between the military and you Politicals!' Ogilvie was bitter, as bitter as he had been back at the train when Wilberforce had been insistent about recovering the gold at whatever risk to the Scots. 'I'll tell you one thing, Harlow: my job's to get those Pathans before they cross back into Afghanistan. Now I know roughly where they are, that's just what I'm going to do!'

'And risk losing the gold?'

'Once I catch up with the Pathans, I'll get the gold as well.'

Harlow pursed his lips. 'I'd advise you not to attempt anything rash, old chap. Calcutta's going to be a damn sight happier with the gold than with a bunch of dead Afghan tribesmen, believe you me!'

The orders had gone forth from Division in Patna and, however crazy those orders might be, they had been obeyed. Native repair gangs were brought together to work under the command of a sapper major, and a large party with their movable equipment and implements was embarked aboard a fleet of very motley craft, including a moth-eaten houseboat, and sailed west for Bundarbar. No one aboard the miniature fleet was under any illusions at all: their journey, if not totally useless, was very premature. Nothing could be done until the floods had subsided, and even then not straight away. The land must be allowed to drain and settle first, for one thing. However, there it was: Lieutenant-General Fettleworth had spoken, over-ruling his Chief of Staff and his advisers from the sappers. Without the gold, the train itself was not vastly important, but one thing stood uppermost in the mind of Bloody Francis: he must be seen by Calcutta to be doing something rather than nothing; he could not possibly envisage sending a report to Calcutta that no action had been taken. There were times for masterly inactivity, certainly; but this was not one of them. So the curious fleet set out, propelled by oars and paddles with the houseboat, like a kind of admiral's flagship, being drawn along at the head by a team of four horses provided by the Supply and Transport of the Indian Army, beasts that plodded valiantly over the flooded land with the water reaching to their bellies and at times becoming so deep that they were forced to swim with curious results to the houseboat.

When Cunningham saw their eventual arrival, still in the distance, he could scarcely believe his own eyes. He lost no time in reporting to General Farrar-Drumm.

'Sir! There is something very odd approaching from the east, sir.'

'Very odd, Cunningham? I call that an incomplete report. Is it the enemy?'

'I doubt it, sir, very much indeed.'

'A friendly force, then?'

'Not a force, sir, I believe. A fleet.'

By this time Farrar-Drumm had managed to extract his binoculars from their case. Thrusting them out of a window, he trained the lenses on the approaching armada and then gave a cackle of laughter. 'Bless my soul, it's a blasted horsedrawn houseboat! And I see uniforms ... Indian Army. Supply and Transport. No doubt from Patna ... Fettleworth must be getting senile – make himself the laughing stock of India.' Farrar-Drumm coughed. 'Yer didn't hear that, Sar'nt-Major.'

'Not a word, sir.'
'I wonder what the idea is?'
'Relief, sir?'
'Well, possibly. I expected General Fettleworth to show concern for me, of course, but I'm not accustomed to be met by the damn Supply and Transport, it's unfitting for a General Officer Commanding, *blasted* unfitting! And a lot of native workmen – ah! Now I see.'
'Sir?'
Farrar-Drumm lowered his glasses. 'A repair detail, Sar'nt-Major. The track, doncher know. They're coming to repair it.'
'While it's still under water, sir?'
'Well, I don't know, I'm not a technical man, thank God. We must not look gift horses in the mouth, Sar'nt-Major. At least we shall be able to move soon after the waters subside, which is a point I believe I have made before. Upon reflection I think General Fettleworth has shown himself a man of vision and forethought.' Farrar-Drumm's tone changed. 'I tell yer one thing, though, Sar'nt-Major – if the idea is for me to be taken on to Patna in that damn floating circus of a houseboat. I shall refuse point-blank, damned if I won't! I'd never live it down when the word reached Ootacamund.'
'Aye, sir. But General Fettleworth may have sailed it specially for you, sir.'

'Then I shall damn well sail it back again!' Farrar-Drumm said energetically, waving his walking-stick. The strange-looking fleet came nearer, very slowly as the arms of the rowers and paddlers grew weary. Stared at with much curiosity from all the windows of the train, the craft entered the station behind the houseboat with its horses. Some attempt at decorum had been made by the sappers and the men from the Supply and Transport: a line of drivers had been drawn up on the houseboat's roof and as the vessel moved past the white head of Sir Clarence Farrar-Drumm thrust from the train window, an officer in khaki called the drivers to attention and saluted.

Farrar-Drumm called out, 'Have yer come to repair the railway line, or what?'

'Yes, sir. Repair, sir.'

'Do yer best, then.'

The houseboat was drawn on a little farther and came to rest at the western end of the station. A rope was led from its bows to a stout post forming part of a fence, and its horses' ropes were cast off from the towing-bitts. From it, into eighteen inches of dirty water, stepped a man in a crumpled white suit and a deplorably dirty white topee. On the man's shoulder sat a monkey, chattering and grinning: Major Blaise-Willoughby, ordered west by Fettleworth to investigate stolen gold bullion, had taken passage aboard the repair fleet; and he now proceeded to report to General Farrar-Drumm in his coach.

'Met yer before,' Farrar-Drumm said disparagingly. He disliked so-called officers who wore dirty white suits, and he disliked the Politicals even when they were clean and tidy. 'I wasn't impressed then, and I'm not now.'

Blaise-Willoughby waved a hand, airily. He was accustomed to the whims of generals and was well enough aware that the fighting officers mistrusted his kind. 'I am not distressed by that, General.'

'Damn well ought to be. Yer could at least have yer blasted clothes decently pressed I should have thought.'

'My appearance is part of my job, my dear sir, and if I looked like a popinjay outside Buckingham Palace I couldn't do my job effectively. Now, sir.' Blaise-Willoughby sat down uninvited. 'I understand you've lost some gold bullion—'

'Lost before my arrival, Major Blaise-Willoughby.'

Blaise-Willoughby nodded. 'Yes, I have a note to that effect. Then let us say you inherited a loss. I take it you've assumed command here?'

'Of course, of course!' Farrar-Drumm said irritably.

'I understand also that Captain Ogilvie of

the 114th Highlanders has gone in search and pursuit of the culprits.'

'The Pathans.'

'Exactly – the culprits.'

Farrar-Drumm glared at the implicit correction. He snapped, 'Oh, call 'em the Pathans, man, like anyone else! In India the word culprit makes 'em sound like yet another blasted tribe!'

Blaise-Willoughby shrugged. 'As you wish, General. The Pathans, then. Has any word been received back from Captain Ogilvie?'

'No. Have any troops been despatched from Patna to my assistance?'

'No, General.'

'Why not?'

Blaise-Willoughby tapped a pencil against his teeth. 'Not my province, General. If I may hazard a guess, it would be that all troops from Division are fully employed on flood relief.'

'Damnfool answer,' Farrar-Drumm muttered. 'There must be some to be spared.' He changed his tack. 'What's that house-boat for? For my accommodation whilst flood-bound?'

'No, no, for the accommodation of the repair gangs.'

'*Natives?* Damn—'

'I suggest we get back to the gold bullion. General.' Blaise-Willoughby sounded bored but firm. Farrar-Drumm considered him a supercilious upstart, but was refraining from saying so. 'General Fettleworth regards the loss as most serious—'

'It doesn't concern me what General Fettleworth regards anything as. I'm not under his command, Major Blaise-Willoughby, and in fact I command a formation larger than his even though my rank is junior to his. Kindly remember that!'

'Yes, of course,' Blaise-Willoughby said obligingly. He went on, 'Although it doesn't concern you, General Fettleworth still takes the most serious view. Although it doesn't concern you, he sends orders that the gold is to be retrieved, though I have to confess he hasn't indicated any thoughts as to how that may be done. Although it doesn't concern you—'

'Shut up!' Farrar-Drumm roared suddenly, his face puce. 'Insolent puppy!' Further words failed him and he subsided, muttering with anger. Blaise-Willoughby took advantage of the mortified silence to press home Fettleworth's wishes in regard to the gold. There was much to be done, and he was there to do it. After certain preliminaries, which would involve an examination of the woodwork of the grenade-shattered guard's van, he, Blaise-Willoughby, would make his way to Chapra where he would find a fellow member of the Political

Service. From a meeting, much might flow.

'And much might damn well not,' Farrar-Drumm said, still angry. 'And what, pray, are these preliminaries and examinations to be?'

Blaise-Willoughby said, 'For one thing, finger-prints—'

'Finger-prints?' Farrar-Drumm gaped incredulously. 'Tommy rot! Tommy rot, I say!' He pounded his walking-stick on the floor of the coach.

'On the contrary, General. It's a well-authenticated process now, and about to be recognised officially as acceptable evidence by the government of India, which is ahead of the home government in that respect—'

'It's still tommy rot. By jove!' Farrar-Drumm grew much excited. 'Yer find these finger-prints, or *perhaps* yer do though I take leave to doubt it, and then yer march throughout Northern Command with yer blasted ink pads, taking down the finger-prints of every blasted Pathan yer find before he shoots yer or cuts yer blasted throat, and compare them with what yer found in the guard's van! Great God above, Blaise-Willoughby, what a way to run an army!'

West of Bundarbar, west of Chapra, the Scots remained on guard throughout the night, still surrounding the small cluster of hovels that formed the village. After midnight, Ogilvie passed word via MacTrease that one man in two could stand down, remaining in his place and sleeping with his rifle in his arms. Ogilvie himself snatched a couple of hours sleep as dawn lit the sky, Harrington taking over meanwhile. He awoke still feeling dead tired, and with a stiffness in his neck and limbs that seemed disinclined to vanish with exercise. He was worried for the future: as yet, no new plan had been worked out. It was expected that the moneychanger, Patel, unaware of the arrival of the Scots, would hold to the plan as originally conceived and would show himself in the vicinity after dark that night, whereupon he would be seized and made to play his part if the Pathans, whose actions could not be forecast, should still come to the village. Harlow was still set firm against any attempt by Ogilvie to march out in search of them. He had made his points well: the Pathans would not be easily found if at all, and Ogilvie would be wasting his time as he had done already in his fruitless march. It would be far better to wait for the Pathans to move, to show themselves perhaps. Even though the pipes and drums would almost certainly have been heard, the Pathans might still feel that the British could be overwhelmed by weight of numbers; if so, Ogilvie's chance for action would come.

'But if we can achieve what we want without action.' Harlow said, 'surely it's better? You've already spoken of casualties to your men. Why not try to avoid more?'

It was, of course, good advice: Ogilvie took it, having a care for his men. Harlow had added that in his opinion nothing would be lost by waiting. The Pathans, he said, were unlikely to go away with the transaction uncompleted. They had already delayed dangerously long and they must know that by now the Frontier would be under heavy watch, with the British patrols guarding the known passes out of the North-West Frontier. They could not rely upon their routes, and they could not risk being brought to action and found with the gold bullion upon them. Rupees were a different story; they could be spread widely amongst the individual tribesmen and were not of themselves incriminating evidence. All this was true; Ogilvie accepted the unwelcome fact that he was going to have to play a waiting game. He considered the possibilities of marching out, withdrawing openly, so that Harlow could revert to his original plan, but realised that the moment his company withdrew there would be contact between the Pathans and the villagers and Harlow's identity as a British agent would be reported to the tribesmen and that would be that.

It was a time for patience.

In the early morning breakfast was cooked on the company stoves and the perimeter guard was kept up as the men detached in groups for the meal. The day passed slowly, beneath a sky that was now wonderfully clear of rain-clouds. The sun began to dry out the damp ground and men's spirits rose with it. There was an air of peace, or there would have been had the villagers not displayed their enmity towards the British who had come to interrupt their daily life and to deprive them of the chance of earning the welcome cut that was to have come from the fat moneychanger in Chapra town. Even the children shunned the soldiers; and those children were another worry for Ogilvie. It was unthinkable that they should be caught in the gunfire if and when the Pathans came. That alone was another argument for his withdrawal; but scarcely one that would commend itself to Calcutta if he marched away and as a result Harlow's plan went astray, as all plans were only too likely to do in the wily sub-continent.

Dusk came down at last, and the Scots stood to with greater vigilance. Now unkind clouds had re-formed and there was no moon. The dark was so intense, so black, as almost to be felt. Ogilvie and MacTrease together patrolled the perimeter, ears and eyes straining.

There was an uncanny feel, an extraordinary sense of total cut-off. A faint breeze came up to whistle ghost-like past the hovels, shaking the trees. And suddenly MacTrease laid a hand on Ogilvie's arm.

'Wheesht, sir,' he said in a low voice, a voice of warning.

'What is it, Colour?'

'A movement, sir. Very faint but unmistakable. D'ye feel it now?'

Ogilvie stood stock still. It was curious in the extreme: something could indeed be felt rather than heard, a kind of inward pressure. Ogilvie realised after a moment that the perimeter was surrounded, that the invisible Pathans were closing in.

Nine

The uncanny silence continued, but after a while was broken by small sounds, the sounds made by the Pathans' bandoliers and the *jezails*. The ground, not entirely dried out yet, muffled the footfalls. By now Ogilvie and MacTrease had passed the word, quietly, to such of the men as had not yet realised what was happening; and at the same time had passed the action orders. Ogilvie started the ball rolling by firing his revolver into the night's darkness. There was no time to listen for a result before all the Scots' rifles crashed out, firing blind as Ogilvie had done.

There were screams and yells and then, as the second volley went in from the Royal Strathspey, followed by another, the Pathans charged the line from all around the perimeter. Many of them were mounted: the screams of wounded and dying horses tore through the night, now lit by the flashes from the rifles and *jezails*. Many of the Scots had fallen, a number of them to the long, snaky bayonets on the *jezails*. But the line, though breached in many places as the wild tribesmen burst through, held in basis; and the Scots lost no time in turning the rifles inwards to pour their bullets into the Pathan mass in the centre. The slaughter was immense; Ogilvie himself despatched two ragged, bearded men who had the Political Officer on the ground and were standing over him with their bayonets poised to drive through his chest and neck. This, Ogilvie saw in the light now streaming from a number of village huts that had been set ablaze by the Pathans; and he fired his revolver point blank into each face in turn. As the tribesmen collapsed over Harlow's body, Ogilvie dragged him clear and set him on his feet.

'Thanks,' Harlow said breathlessly.

Ogilvie said, 'You'd better stick with me. D'you suppose they've come largely to get you?'

'It's highly possible – since they must have known about your soldiers coming in. They'll be blaming me for that.'

'Would they recognise you?'

'I doubt it. They'll just hope to get me with the rest of the village. How's it going, in the broad sense?'

'Not too badly. We have them surrounded. On the other hand—'

'They're in greater numbers?'

'Yes. But I'm not too worried. We've accounted for a good proportion of them already.' Ogilvie dodged nimbly as a *jezail* was turned on him: the bullet smacked into the wall of a hut behind him. He fired back before the man could come in with his bayonet, and the Pathan went down in a writhing heap on the ground. By now the Scots seemed to be getting the advantage: as ever, the clumsy *jezails* took much too long to reload, and in this kind of battle that counted for a lot to the Pathans' disfavour.

Major Blaise-Willoughby had left the halted train at Bundarbar, sped on his way by more derisive references to finger-printing and allied subjects; General Farrar-Drumm was no believer in anything fangled since the damn Zulu War. The new ideas just went to prove how namby-pamby the modern generation was. In his younger day, miscreants had been run to earth, hunted down by much more straightforward and less sneaky methods than dipping their fingers in messy ink and splodging them onto a piece of paper. Besides, you had to catch the buggers first ... it was all damn stupid! He had said so; and Blaise-Willoughby, after completing his examination of the remains of the guard's van, and finding no fingerprints, enquired of the General if he wished to be given transport on to Patna to rejoin his staff and troops and take up his command again.

'There *is* the houseboat,' Blaise-Willoughby said doubtfully, 'though I understand it would be inconvenient since, as I said, the repair gangs are using it—'

'They may continue to do so, thank you, Major Blaise-Willoughby, since I intend to remain here. There is a need of me, to succour the women and children of the blasted Civilians. I shall not be found wanting in my duty and I am surprised that you should suggest I desert.'

'Please yourself. General,' Blaise-Willoughby said with a shrug. Leaving Farrar-Drumm's furious presence, he had set out for Chapra, ferried across the flood to the water's end in a small boat propelled by two *sepoys* from an Indian regiment attached to General Fettleworth's division. Wolseley, in a bad state of nervous excitement on account of the surrounding water, went with his master. It took a long while to reach Chapra, the last part of the journey having to be made on foot; the darkness had descended when Blaise-Willoughby reached the town and headed on for the British Residency, where Humphrey Pollinger, called away from pre-dinner-party *chota pegs*, had news, relevant news that had just come to hand: Harlow, the local political man, had left Chapra for the village of

Dassar and Pollinger believed it very possible that his journey had to do with the stolen gold bullion. Dassar might be worth a visit.

Blaise-Willoughby, knowing that Dassar was all of twenty miles to the west of Chapra, mentioned his lack of transport.

'Oh, that's all right.' Pollinger waved a cigar in the air. 'I have mules – you're very welcome to one.'

'I'd sooner have a horse.'

Pollinger grinned. 'Who wouldn't? I'm sorry, but it's a mule or nothing. That's how we're placed ... Calcutta's getting somewhat cheese-paring these days.'

'Oh, very well.' Blaise-Willoughby lifted a hand and patted Wolseley's reddish-brown fur. 'By the way, have you telegraphed this news through to Patna?'

'No,' Pollinger said. 'The lines are down – cursed nuisance, but there it is – just happened. The local banditry, you know. And we're still out of communication with Bundarbar as you're aware, not that that would help in the circumstances—'

'Quite. Then what—'

'I'm about to telegraph Nowshera. The lines are all right in that direction. I think they ought to know about Harlow, in case the question of assistance arises.'

'Nowshera's a devil of a long way off!'

'It's all I can do,' Pollinger said with a

shrug.

Blaise-Willoughby gave a gloomy nod. He said, 'I understand a Scots captain named Ogilvie – Sir Iain's son, you know – is somewhere in the vicinity. Do you know anything of his movements?'

'He reported here on arrival,' Pollinger said. 'He marched out again soon after, heading west. That's all I know.'

Blaise-Willoughby frowned: he could only hope Ogilvie would not be ham-handed. It was not a confrontation that was needed, in Blaise-Willoughby's view; this was a case of softly, softly catchee monkey. The infantry was not much good at that.

Pollinger provided a meal, though this was not taken with the Residency guests: Blaise-Willoughby preferred the privacy of Pollinger's study, where he munched gloomily in company with Wolseley, who ate the leftovers. There was a bottle of good French wine, just off the ice; of this Blaise-Willoughby left but little behind. After the meal, the mule was brought by a *syce* to the Residency compound, together with sustaining rations to keep Blaise-Willoughby going whilst upon his lonely fact-finding trek; also water-bottles. These were stowed in leather saddle-bags.

Blaise-Willoughby set off, after learning that there was currently a difficulty in getting Pollinger's message through to Nowshera. Blaise-Willoughby was less worried about this than about the mule. He was not good with mules at the best of times; in his regimental days, mule transport had been his greatest bugbear. For some time the beast, after leaving Chapra fairly docilely, had refused to move an inch and when pulled by its bridle had dug its feet in firmly. Then it had relented and walked forward; and Blaise-Willoughby had taken advantage of its change of mood to mount. The mule, after some two dozen delicate paces forward, had gone suddenly berserk, though fortunately in the right direction for Dassar, belting off at enormous speed. Blaise-Willoughby, after a very dangerous teeter backwards, had managed to cling on for quite some way. But not all the way; suddenly changing its tactics once again after some miles of torment for its rider, the mule had abruptly stopped, and Blaise-Willoughby had sailed right over its ears to land with boneshaking, winding force in a bush. Wolseley had gone with him and had clung on by some miracle known only to monkeys; but was viciously upset by its experiences, enough to make him bite Blaise-Willoughby's ear, from which blood poured.

'Little bastard!' Blaise-Willoughby said furiously. He clambered to his feet and brushed down the white suit, which was more deplorable than ever and now very bloodstained. The mule had gone, he knew not where, and it had taken his provisions and his water-bottles with it. Close to tears of sheer fury and frustration, Blaise-Willoughby paced around in the darkness trying to reorientate himself. It did not, in fact, take him long to pick up the track; and, observing, by the light of a watery moon that shone for a brief and lucky moment through the clouds, the hoofmarks of the mule on its outward journey from Chapra, he was able to point his footsteps in the right direction for Dassar. He had been walking for three hours by his watch when he saw, ahead and distantly, the flicker of fire, red and angry. He had seen such fires before: a village was being burned to the ground, and on this occasion Blaise-Willoughby doubted if the burning was being done by the soldiers of the Raj. Blaise-Willoughby hurried on. He had a suspicion the fires were in fact dying down; the act was complete. Blaise-Willoughby prayed that nothing had been done that would adversely affect his mission. The recovery of the gold was as important to his personal status as it was to the Raj.

'Colour MacTrease!'

'Sir!' MacTrease, firing rapid rounds from

behind the shelter of an unburned hut, turned.

'They're retreating, Colour. Look at that!'

Ogilvie pointed: the scene was brilliantly lit by the fires. The Pathans were streaming away through a gap in the perimeter line, a gap that was filled by dead and wounded Scots. The Pathans' feet and the hooves of their horses trampled the bodies as they fled. More bullets swept into them, and they pressed on faster. Soon the burning village was empty of the tribesmen; MacTrease was all for pursuit, but Ogilvie vetoed this.

'No use, Colour. They're still mostly mounted, and they'll be carrying those without horses.'

'We could get a few of the buggers, sir!'

'Not enough – not worth more casualties to the Jocks. We've suffered enough as it is.' Ogilvie looked around in the fires' light. He caught his breath at the scale of what in effect had been a small engagement – one company of infantry against perhaps two hundred Pathans. The dead, the dying and the wounded, British and Pathan, lay everywhere; the villagers themselves had largely vanished, fleeing with their children into the darkness while the fighting had been going on. Ogilvie ordered the fit soldiers to remain standing to; MacTrease, carrying out a quick muster, reported thirty-seven casualties, twenty of them fatal. The wounds were mostly superficial, but they could count on three more deaths within hours in the absence of medical attention.

'A sad story, sir.' MacTrease sucked at a hollow tooth, his face grim. 'However, there's the bright side, I suppose: there's near on a hundred o' the bloody Pathans left behind, and most of the buggers dead.'

Ogilvie nodded. He said in a hard voice, 'Find one of the wounded, Colour. Bring him to me.'

MacTrease looked at him, eyebrows raised. 'Questioning, sir?'

'Yes.'

MacTrease grinned. 'I'll choose you one personally, sir!' He marched away, felt the sog of blood on his kilt: a bayonet had cut across his thigh and he hadn't even noticed it while the fight was on. Now, it hurt. MacTrease shrugged; others were worse off. Halting, he pulled off his tunic, then his shirt. He put the tunic back on and ripped the shirt into strips. He went to the perimeter and found a section sergeant.

'Sar'nt Dunnett?'

'Aye, Colour-Sar'nt?'

'Here.' MacTrease thrust a strip of shirt cloth at him. 'A tourniquet round my thigh, just below the buttocks. And quickly, for I've work to do.'

Sergeant Dunnett fashioned a rough tourniquet with the aid of a bayonet and

MacTrease walked stiffly away when the job was done to make a search of the wounded Pathans, pushing at them with his rifle, turning them over unceremoniously, looking for one who seemed more likely than others to talk, either because of sore wounds or because his face had not the hardness and fanaticism of his comrades. He selected one who appeared to fill both attributes at once, a young Pathan whose eyes lacked the usual fire and whose mouth was bubbling with frothy blood coughed up from a bullet-torn lung.

MacTrease bent and seized the man's shoulders in a hard, unrelenting grip. 'On your feet,' he said, using Pushtu. 'You're for questioning by the Captain sahib – and mind well you don't tell any lies!'

More blood flowed from the mouth: the eyes were pools of agony. MacTrease felt no sorrow: too many of his own company, men he had trained, encouraged, punished for small misdemeanours or nurse-maided into their first action, now lay dead, or wounded like this one. MacTrease urged the Pathan on at the point of his bayonet, approaching Ogilvie, who was talking to Harlow.

'Sir! A prisoner, sir!'

'Thank you, Colour.' Ogilvie spoke to the Pathan, as MacTrease had done, in Pushtu. 'Why did you come to this village, to kill and burn? Tell me this, and your life may be spared. If you do not, then you will hang outside the civil jail in Chapra.' There was no answer. Ogilvie asked, 'Do you understand what I said?'

'I understand.'

'Then answer me. Tell me what your objective was. This was a peaceful village, dwelt in by peaceful men. What brought the bullet and the bayonet upon it in the dead of night?'

There was a silence. Ogilvie caught MacTrease's eye. MacTrease cleared his throat and said, 'Asking's little use, sir. There must be something stronger. With respect, sir. Many of our men have died this night. They should not do that in vain, sir.'

'Yes, Colour, I know. But this man's dead on his feet. To do anything—'

'Just leave him to me, sir. I know well what to do.'

Ogilvie's breath hissed out through his teeth, sharply. He was faced with a difficult decision. Up to a point MacTrease was right. But it went against the grain to inflict, or allow to be inflicted, further suffering on any man so close to death and in mortal agony already. He said, 'No. I'll ask more questions, Colour.'

'As you say, sir.' MacTrease had answered stiffly; his face said that in his opinion Ogilvie was wrong. Ogilvie was about to start the questioning again, preferring to try bribes rather than threats of physical pain, when there was a shout from the eastern perimeter.

'Colour-Sar'nt ... there's someone coming in!'

MacTrease doubled in the direction of the call, letting the Pathan drop to the ground. Ogilvie ran behind the Colour-Sergeant, and, in the flicker of the dying fires, saw a man, staggering with exhaustion, dressed in a dirty white suit. MacTrease, also seeing the man, clicked his tongue and turned back to Ogilvie.

'Major Blaise-Willoughby from Division, sir, plus bloody monkey ... beggin' your pardon, sir.'

Ogilvie grinned at his Colour-Sergeant's tone: The Divisional Political Officer was only too well-known to the rank and file as well as to the officers.

Ten

Blaise-Willoughby was in a nasty mood; the night had been an unpleasant one, and he was far from pleased to find the Scots in the village of Dassar. After greeting his fellow officer from the Political Service he turned on Ogilvie.

'Trust the regimental officers to bugger things up,' he said bitterly. 'Just look at this place!' Blaise-Willoughby swept an arm around the burned-out huts, at the bodies lying on the ground, at the few remaining native inhabitants clustered at one end of the shattered village. 'You're going to have some explaining to do, Ogilvie. Calcutta doesn't like unnecessary pillage, you know—'

'Pillage my foot!' Ogilvie snapped. 'The village was attacked and I defended it, that's all. I suggest you listen to your friend Harlow before you open your mouth again, Major Blaise-Willoughby.'

'All right, all right, no need to fly off the handle.' Blaise-Willoughby gave him a cool stare, then turned to Harlow. 'Well, Roger, perhaps you'll be good enough to explain?'

Harlow did so; Blaise-Willoughby listened, stroking Wolseley meanwhile. He said, 'This man Lakshni Patel. Do I take it he hasn't turned up here?'

'You do,' Harlow answered.

'I suppose he was scared off,' Blaise-Willoughby said, staring at Ogilvie with an eyebrow raised. 'Well, that seems to finish your little stratagem, Roger. Something tells me we start all over again, and not from a very good base at that.'

Ogilvie said, 'Suppose Patel didn't leave Chapra at all?'

'What makes you think he didn't?' Harlow asked.

'Major Blaise-Willoughby came along the track from Chapra. He might have been presumed to have fallen in with anyone coming here, or turning back from here to Chapra – mightn't he?'

'Well, I didn't,' Blaise-Willoughby said, 'but I don't see that it proves anything. Patel would have beaten it off the track if he heard anyone approaching. However, I take your point, Ogilvie: *if* he never left Chapra at all, then he's up to something on his own account. Or he got cold feet at the last – though from what I've heard of Lakshni Patel, the prospect of adding to his riches has always over-ridden his fears.' He paused, frowning and biting at his lip. 'I tell you one thing: wherever Patel is now and in the immediate future, he won't be at his home address!'

'Quite,' Harlow said. 'And he'll be making very sure his tracks are covered.'

'You know your territory, Roger. What would be the chances of rooting him out?'

Harlow shrugged. 'Damn small. All Chapra will shut its collective mouth. Patel's said to have a million tentacles, all with a tight stranglehold where it matters.'

'In other words it would take time?'

'Too much time,' Harlow answered. 'Those Pathans aren't going to linger now. My guess would be they're already riding for the Frontier.'

Blaise-Willoughby nodded, then looked around at the dead and wounded once again; the fires were almost out, the huts no more than a red glow of ashes, but the sky was lightening to the dawn. 'Anyone tried questioning some of these buggers?' Blaise-Willoughby asked.

Ogilvie said, 'Yes, but without result.'

'Really! Which one?'

Ogilvie gestured towards the young Pathan, lying crumpled at MacTrease's feet. Blaise-Willoughby said, 'H'm. Uncooperative, was he?'

Ogilvie nodded.

'I'll have a go at him,' Blaise-Willoughby said, a hard light visible in his eyes. 'I have a trick or two up my sleeve.'

'Dirty ones, I suppose, Major?'

Blaise-Willoughby stared at Ogilvie. He said, 'There's no need for you to become involved. I'm not even asking your permission. I carry my own authority. All I ask of you is that you withdraw your men to the other end of the village and leave me with that Pathan ... for as long as it takes. All right?'

Bloody Francis Fettleworth was in an agitated state: there was so much to do, so many details to think about. The floods had largely left Patna by this time and he had been on the point of moving out his division in accordance with his earlier orders to advance to the east when the telegraph had started up from Calcutta and seemed never to stop; one order had come through after another – orders from the Commander-in-Chief, orders from His Excellency the Viceroy, orders originating from that bane of any foreign-serving general's very existence, Whitehall. Fettleworth found himself virtually sitting to attention at his trestle table as the messages came through from all these important persons. The gist of it all was simple enough, to be sure: the missing gold bullion had shaken Calcutta badly and it now took precedence of flood relief. The First Division was not now to march east, but was to march west. Everything was, in effect, to be put into reverse. As his Chief of Staff remarked, to Bloody Francis' irritation, there was a strong element of the Good Old Duke of York, who had marched his men to the top of the hill, then marched them down again. Fettleworth was to take his division towards Bundarbar, the scene of the daring robbery; and simultaneously Nowshera had been ordered – over Fettleworth's head in his absence from his base – to despatch its cavalry formations eastwards without delay.

'I don't see the damn *point*!' Fettleworth stormed at Lakenham.

'The telegraph was clear enough, I fancy. The object is to pincer the Pathans ... the cavalry from the west, us from the east. Each of us will, as it were, drive the Pathans towards the other, and—'

'Yes, yes, yes!' Fettleworth dabbed at his cheeks with a handkerchief: Patna was abominably hot and close, a dreadful place. 'I understand that! But why denude the damn Frontier of its cavalry patrols, Lakenham? Surely to God that's the very way to open up the blasted passes for the Pathans to escape through, isn't it?'

Lakenham answered patiently. 'I think not, sir. The messages were clear on that point also, if you remember: the cavalry at Mardan will be left upon the Frontier to carry on the patrols – reduced, admittedly – and Sir Iain Ogilvie will mount extended patrols from Murree and Rawalpindi to cover Waziristan. I really don't think you need worry. Sir George White knows what he's doing, after all.'

'I sometimes wonder,' Fettleworth said moodily. 'He's no longer a young man, you know.' He drummed his fingers on the trestle table, feeling distraught. Other urgent messages had come: General Farrar-Drumm's Southern Army currently in Patna minus its Commander was to be ordered to deploy to the south, then march west below Bundarbar to cut off the Pathans from that direction, extending north in due course, and God knew what *that* might mean, to add to the pincer grip on the marauders. It was all thoroughly confusing, Fettleworth thought. Naturally, he understood the importance of the gold bullion, not for its intrinsic value alone, but also and in a sense more vitally for the moral effect upon the Raj if the buggers should get away with it, laughing all the way to Kabul once they'd crossed the North-West Frontier. That could not be allowed and Fettleworth conceded the point ... but such a fuss and bother! For solace he lifted his eyes to gaze upon his travelling portrait of Her Majesty the Queen-Empress, hanging currently from a coat-hook, very slightly askew, set into the wall opposite him above his thunderbox, for which, in the overcrowded condition of his makeshift headquarters, no other apartment could be found. Fettleworth glowered: provision would have to be made for his thunderbox on the march, another damn detail which very likely Lakenham hadn't yet thought about. Fettleworth's colour deepened a little as he realised he was committing something not far short of treason in even so much as thinking about thunderboxes whilst contemplating the Empress of India, and he shut his mind to the former, concentrating again upon the more regal aspect of his view. The good old Queen ... she was his mainstay here in the farthest-flung part of her Empire. Every inch a ruler: the severe bun, the neat lace cap, the downturned mouth, the ample motherly breast, the expression that some said was slightly disagreeable but which Fettleworth found imperious and sustaining in his daily task of commanding Her Majesty's First Division of the British Army in India, a noble-sounding appointment if ever there was one. And yet – here came unbidden another treasonable thought – Her Majesty had an easier time of it than had her generals. Not so much damn detail.

'Lakenham.'

'Yes, sir?'

'Is everything ready for our move west?'
'I shall report when that is so, sir.'
'Stores, ammunition, transport, field kitchens, shelter-tents, tents for the officers, officers' mess fittings—'
'It will be done, sir—'
'Boot cleaning materials. I much dislike dirty boots and all boots must be polished daily. See to that, Lakenham – issue repeat orders on the point, some of the adjutants get damn slack if you don't say everything ten times. Puttees to be kept tight at all times. Socks to be switched each morning from left foot to right and vice versa – half the time the men take no damn notice of the Field Service Pocket Book and then they complain about sore feet. I won't have it. And what about General Farrar-Drumm, may one ask?'
Lakenham lifted his eyebrows. '*What* about him, sir?'
'Is he still sitting on his backside in that train at Bundarbar?'
'According to the latest information, yes.'
'Then we shall meet, I suppose.'
'Yes, sir.'
'Damn!'

Two hours later, the First Division was ready to move out; cumbersomely, it did so. In the van rode Bloody Francis Fettleworth on a makeshift charger found for him by the

Supply and Transport, a beast that by clandestine request of the Chief of Staff was the least mettlesome to be found, since the Divisional Commander was a poor horseman and liable to be thrown at the drop of a hat. Just as the whole unwieldy column was about to move off, Fettleworth remembered the Queen's Own Royal Strathspey.

'Lakenham, the 114th Highlanders!'

'On special service, sir, the main body spreading disinfectants to prevent disease, one company detached to Bundarbar and thence—'

'Yes, yes, yes! What I mean is, don't you damn well see, what fresh orders have been given to them as a result of our move west?'

'None, sir. None at all.'

'Great God, why not?'

Lakenham blew out a long, hissing breath. 'Because orders cannot be transmitted to the thin air, sir!'

'What do you mean by that, pray?'

'We have no knowledge as to the present whereabouts of the 114th. That is what I mean.'

'Yes, we have – in a broad sense.'

'Too broad for orders to reach them. They are in the field, sir!'

'Kindly don't be impertinent, Lakenham.'

'I'm sorry, sir. I dare say mounted runners could be sent to – to *scour* the countryside and convey orders.' The Chief of Staff paused. 'Have you particular orders in mind for the 114th?'

'No!' Fettleworth snapped. Lakenham gave an eloquent shrug and the column proceeded on its way west across the desolate landscape, grey and filthy from the flood's aftermath and reeking of death and decay. After some half-hour's progress towards Bundarbar, Bloody Francis changed his mind. He had, he said, orders for the Royal Strathspey after all, or if not orders precisely, then strategic intelligence: Lord Dornoch was to be warned to be on the watch for marauding Pathans bearing gold, and trying to evade the vengeance of the Raj. This warning should have been sent earlier, and Lakenham should have thought of it. Mounted runners were now to be sent on the scouring mission suggested with tongue in cheek by the Chief of Staff. They would scour along the general line of advance of the Scots as ordered before the battalion had marched out from Patna earlier.

Blaise-Willoughby took his time, even though time might be short: the Raj must not be seen to be agitated. Calmness and patience indicated an inbred certainty of victory; and victory was what Blaise-Willoughby achieved in the end, and apparently achieved it by words alone. At any rate there were no screams and when the Political

Officer called Ogilvie back there were no visible signs of physical duress even though the young tribesman's eyes were wide with fear as they stared at Blaise-Willoughby with a terrible intensity. Blaise-Willoughby looked extremely pleased with himself and was smiling broadly.

'Well?' Ogilvie asked.

'Very well indeed! He's talked, Ogilvie. My methods were the better, you see. All the same, you chose well to pick a youngster – but I won't go into all that. What he said – that's the important thing, isn't it?'

'What did he say, Major?'

'The Pathans didn't trust Lakshni Patel, it seems. They suspected they might meet trouble in the village, that he would have his henchmen handy. So they intercepted him not far out from Chapra.'

'And?'

Blaise-Willoughby spread his hands wide. 'And they took his rupees, and they killed him. The normal Pathan reaction. So now they have both the rupees—'

'Forged ones,' Harlow put in.

'Oh, no doubt, but not without value to those who fail to recognise them as such. They have the rupees *and* the gold. They attacked the village because they heard you marching in, Ogilvie, and believed you might be on their track. So they decided to wipe out your company, or try to.'

'What's their next move to be – did you find that out?'

Blaise-Willoughby shook his head. 'No. The boy didn't know – at least, not in any precise sense. But I did get the impression they're playing it warily. They know very well they've set the Raj by the ears, and that the Raj will use every endeavour to stop them crossing the Frontier into Afghanistan. Therefore, contrary I have to admit to my own theory, they're not going to try to cross just yet. They're lying low in the hills to the north of here, the sort of country they feel at home in and the gold's very well guarded. They're well provisioned and armed, and they can remain where they are for long enough – that's their belief, anyway. And I suggest, Ogilvie, that you refrain from putting it to the test.'

'You mean, don't attack?'

'Exactly,' Blaise-Willoughby answered. 'You wouldn't have a hope in any case. According to my Pathan, there's around five to six hundred of them. It would be useless to attack with less than battalion strength at the very least, and for my money, considering their defensive situation, a brigade would be needed.' He paused. 'The nearest brigade's in Patna. Some way!'

'My regiment's probably nearer, but I don't know its exact location—'

'Forget it, then. Anyway, I repeat, a

brigade, no less, is what's wanted, Ogilvie. If we can get word through to the Resident in Chapra, he may be back in telegraph communication with Patna. If not, the word'll have to be taken on by mounted runner. I'm willing to take the message through to Chapra – anything would be better than staying in this Godforsaken dump!' Blaise-Willoughby looked around at the bodies. Overhead the vultures had been clustering for some while, hovering and swooping but kept from their prey by the British bullets that scattered them when they came too close. The burials would have to be made quickly; the sun was up by now and there could not be much more delay. Blaise-Willoughby gave a slight shudder. Despite his slovenly appearance, he was a fastidious man on some counts. As Ogilvie made no response to his offer to walk all the way back to Chapra, Blaise-Willoughby said, 'Well, there we are, then. I'll start at once. The sooner the better.'

Ogilvie said, 'You'd never get there, Major. The moment the Pathans see anyone leave the village, they'll be down on him like a ton of bricks.'

'Well, that's a point.' Blaise-Willoughby looked angry at being reminded of what he should have taken into account: Ogilvie was only too right. 'After dark, then. Pity about the delay, but I dare say, in the light of this new information, we have time in hand yet.' He gave a cough and gestured towards the dead. 'I suggest a speedy burial, Ogilvie. You know what India's like.'

'Yes,' Ogilvie said shortly. He moved away and had a word with MacTrease. Parties were detailed and graves dug for the Scots. The Pathans were carried away to be left for the vultures, who departed with eager beaks and hoarse cries of anticipation for the heap of food; within minutes they could clearly be heard, tugging at the flesh until beak met bone. When the graves were dug, Ogilvie read a simple service as Farrar-Drumm had done at Bundarbar, and the graves were filled in and the surrounding land searched for all the stones that could be found to build the lonely cairns that would mark another chapter in the history of the Raj. The day wore on with only picquets posted now; any advance from the hills in daylight would be spotted in good time for the men to stand to. The sun grew high and then declined into a splendid, many-coloured sunset, upon which Blaise-Willoughby made ready to leave for Chapra. It would be a gruellingly long walk; Blaise-Willoughby couldn't arrive before breakfast-time next day, if then. And after that it would be up to the telegraph, or himself upon a horse if such could be found for him in Chapra: no more mules. He had already left the perimeter when MacTrease marched up to Ogilvie and saluted.

'Major Blaise-Willoughby's too late, sir. I hear horsemen approaching.'

So did Blaise-Willoughby; he came back into the village at the double, clutching his topee. No news, no request for reinforcements, would leave Dassar that night. The sound of hooves was loud now as the Scots worked the bolts of their rifles, sending the bullets up the spout in readiness for what was coming.

Eleven

Lord Dornoch, standing by his tent after the 114th Highlanders, moving west from Patna, had gone once again into night bivouacs, also saw the splendid sunset, red and gold, orange and green. The Colonel knocked out his pipe, and sighed. He was weary, and he was sick at heart: India could be beautiful, but was always cruel to its inhabitants, at any rate the lowly ones. In the last day or two Dornoch had seen far too much suffering for his peace of mind. There had been flood, now before long there would be famine as a direct result. Many thousands of villagers had been drowned, and their bodies had rotted as the regiment had marched on its mercy mission, spreading its disinfectant and bringing in the medical supplies and the attentions of the attached doctors and their orderlies from Division. Whole families had been decimated, though perhaps the saddest cases were those where only the children had survived, to struggle as orphans for their daily bread and for their lives. It had been heart-rending: Dornoch used the word to the Major as Brora approached him beneath that superb sunset.

'I don't know about heart-rending,' Brora said, and gave a laugh. 'Damned smelly – that's what strikes me most! As a matter of fact, most of them are better off dead. They've never had much and what you haven't got you don't miss.'

Dornoch bent and quite unnecessarily knocked out his pipe again: he didn't want Brora to read the dislike in his eyes. He asked, 'And you don't find *that* heart-rending, Major?'

'Certainly not! Should I?'

Dornoch said quietly, 'They've lived such wretched lives – that's what I find sad. No pleasure – and then this!'

'It's their lot in life. Untouchables, sweepers ... why disturb yourself about them, Colonel? They accept what they've been given, and I doubt if they grudge what others have.'

'Then they ought to. The wealth of some of the princes is disgusting, quite disgraceful by contrast. Rooms full of rubies, diamonds, emeralds, gold! I've seen them myself. Half of that could be stripped away and still leave them the world's richest men.'

'You speak like a damned Socialist, Colonel.'

'For which I make no apology tonight!'

'Are you going to take your socialism back to Scotland, Colonel, and have your domestics and your gardeners and ghillies treat themselves as your equal, and question your orders?'

Dornoch smiled icily. 'You are a man of little sensibility, I fear, Major, and I shall say goodnight—'

'A moment first, if you please, Colonel.' Brora's voice was harsh, his high-cheekboned face arrogant. 'If I may take up a little of your time, I wish to raise the matter of my niece and my sister-in-law.'

'Very well,' Dornoch said after a pause.

'There has been no news, and I am naturally anxious. I would have thought Ogilvie could have sent word—'

'He has no means of knowing where we are, Major.'

'Then he could damn well use his initiative and find means of his own,' Brora said harshly, slapping his cane down the leg of his tartan trews. 'A battalion is never exactly inconspicuous, I would have thought. Now, the fact that he has not made contact with us could be due to his own stupid lack of resources, or it could be because his company has come under attack – with unfortunate results. You, I realise well, do not consider Ogilvie to lack ability, or to be stupid. Thus I put it to you, with respect, Colonel, that you can only agree that he has marched into trouble, and that trouble may—'

'Yes, very well, Major, that'll do.' Brora had begun to sound over-excited, bordering, not for the first time, on a kind of hysteria. Dornoch went on, 'Of course there could have been fighting – I agree—'

'I'm glad, Colonel, that we see eye to eye on that point. In that case, you'll perhaps detach runners to Bundarbar, and find out what the situation is?'

Dornoch shook his head. 'I've considered it, and rejected it.'

'I see. May I ask why, Colonel?'

'Because it's not long since Ogilvie's company detached, and I don't propose to send any man into danger unnecessarily, that's why. Runners could be much at risk.'

'So is my niece and my sister-in-law.'

'They have the protection of Ogilvie's company, Major, which Division considered strength enough. So do I. It's much too soon to start panicking simply because we have no news, and I shall not send runners to Bundarbar.'

'If you will not, then I ask leave to go myself.'

Dornoch, about to utter a sharp rebuke for a foolish request, paused. Brora was a confounded nuisance at the best of times, and on this mission he had proved impossible. It was his nature to fight, to wield his broadsword against an enemy; he had refused to co-operate in the war on germs and in trying to bring succour to the homeless people of the villages. The battalion would be much better off without him, much more able to perform its duty. So instead of an outright refusal, Dornoch asked, 'Is that a serious request, Major?'

'Yes, by God, it is, Colonel!'

'If you go, you go knowing the risks involved—'

'The devil take the risks, Colonel, I'm no damn coward.'

'No, I know that to be true. But you go as the result of your own request, not by my order. Is that quite clear?'

'Quite clear, Colonel.'

'Very well, then. You may detach for Bundarbar. I shall expect you back with your report by tomorrow's sunset, unless you find yourself needed by Ogilvie, in which case you may remain.'

'Thank you, Colonel. I shall lose no time – I shall ride at once.' Brora turned and marched away, shouting for his *syce* to bring his horse. Lord Dornoch stared after him, already wondering if he had made a mistake in acceding to the Major's request. In a sense it had been a natural request, though Brora had hitherto shown scant concern for his womenfolk; but Dornoch had more than a suspicion that the Major's real motive was to place himself between Ogilvie and his niece. As to his own motives in allowing Brora to go, Dornoch feared that he had acted in self-interest, a result of that sheer desire to be relieved of his second-in-command. In so doing, he was undoubtedly delivering an incubus to sit around Ogilvie's neck ... that was regrettable, of course, but the die was cast now.

The following morning, word of an incoming force reached General Farrar-Drumm at Bundarbar. The news was brought by Cunningham, who reported that General Fettleworth's division was approaching the train.

'Bother take it!' Farrar-Drumm exclaimed. 'Are you quite sure it's General Fettleworth, Sar'nt-Major?'

'Quite sure, sir. The divisional standard is very familiar to me, sir.'

'Yes, I suppose it is. What a blasted nuisance! Where's my ADC?'

'Here, sir,' said Captain Smyth from behind him.

'Ah, Smyth. My bugler.'

'At once, sir.' Captain Smyth hesitated. 'There will be a difficult question of protocol, sir—'

'Why's that, pray?'

Smyth said diffidently, 'Lieutenant-General Fettleworth, sir—'

'Yes, yes, and I'm a major-general. I'm aware of that. Where's the difficulty, Smyth?'

'Well, sir, the ranks—'

'Oh, what dashed nonsense, Smyth, I command an army, Fettleworth only a division. He salutes me.' Farrar-Drumm winced as the rheumatic affliction in his legs gave him a nasty twinge. 'Put my bugler on the roof of my coach, if you please, with orders to return General Fettleworth's salute when he sounds off. It's to be done smartly. Fettleworth shall see what we're made of in Southern Army, damned if he shan't.'

The orders were passed, and the bugler ascended with some difficulty to the train's roof and stood in the at-ease position. Immediately below him, as General Fettleworth's cohorts advanced upon the railway station, General Farrar-Drumm thrust his white hair through the window, this time surmounted by his gold-laced field service cap with its scarlet band behind the badge of the General Staff. Then he began coughing and seemed quite unable to stop. Phlegm rumbled and boiled in his chest and throat. He was forced to spit but it failed to do much good. There was plenty more down below. Farrar-Drumm's face grew redder and redder behind and below the facial and head hair. It was very embarrassing. In rear, Captain Smyth asked if he might assist. General Farrar-Drumm was unable to answer, but thrust a hand behind his body and made shooing motions with it. Smyth took the hint and shut his mouth. Outside the train General Fettleworth, in the van of his advance and riding nobly but with his usual poor seat, came closer. He pointed his riding-crop at the face in the train window.

'That's Farrar-Drumm, isn't it?' he asked.

Lakenham said, 'Yes, sir.'

'He looks unwell. He's much too old for an active command, Lakenham. Where's my bugler?'

'All ready, sir.'

'Ensure that he plays his instrument tunefully. The First Division will show old Farrar-Drumm that we're a damn sight smarter in the north than down in Ootacamund.' Fettleworth paused. 'Farrar-Drumm should have saluted me by now, Lakenham.'

'I'm not sure that he should or will, sir. Major-General Farrar-Drumm commands Southern Army, whereas you—'

'Damn it all, I'm a lieutenant-general, Lakenham! It's quite obvious who should salute who and I'm buggered if I'm going to salute first.'

The advance continued, stared at from the train windows by the Civilians and their families. A cheer went up, and excited arms were waved. One small child bore a Union

Flag, which was manna to Fettleworth. But there was no salute; the bugler on the roof of the train had come to attention, but that was all. Fettleworth's bugler, now marching ahead of his General's horse, was all ready but had not yet been told to place his bugle to his lips. Angrily, Fettleworth lifted his right hand to bring the First Division to a halt. Then he called ahead to Farrar-Drumm: 'I am expecting your salute, General.'

There was a loud rumble from the train and Farrar-Drumm, in attempting to speak, spat again instead. Then he vanished.

As soon as Sir Clarence was fit, there were more serious matters to be discussed than the non-exchange of salutes, as to which both generals felt they had drawn even. Fettleworth apprised Farrar-Drumm of the fact that he had ordered Southern Army out from Patna.

Sir Clarence was furious. 'Yer had no damn right! No damn right at all, to give *any* orders to my army!'

'Not my orders, General, but the Commander-in-Chief's.'

'Oh.'

'He wished your army to deploy to the south, to act, as I take it, as a last resort—'

'Damn cheek!'

'Well, as a long-stop, then,' Fettleworth

amended irritably. 'To trap those Pathans with the gold if they try to head that way, which in my view is doubtful – in fact Southern Army is under orders to push westwards, standing as it were to the south of my own advance—'

'Sledgehammer to crack a nut,' Farrar-Drumm observed, still sounding cross.

'Oh, by no means, the gold is vitally important! Those buggers must not be allowed to get away with that sort of thing, General.'

'I still say it's a sledgehammer to crack a nut,' Farrar-Drumm said obstinately. 'All that's needed is a spearhead, something fast with no fat: cavalry. Cavalry, my dear sir!' He slammed a fist into his palm.

'H'm. I've never set much store by cavalry, they're a dunderheaded lot, very stupid—'

'In my regimental days, I was in Her Majesty's Fourth Dragoons.'

'Really? Yes. Well, some like cavalry and some don't. I don't. Same with the guns, they're pretty useless too, always firing at the wrong target. I'm an infantryman – Queen of Battles! Do you know what I would do with my division if we were to be attacked here? I'd form square, right round the train and the station! Nothing would get through my square.'

'Cavalry would,' Farrar-Drumm said grumpily.

'The Duke of Wellington said—'

‘What’s that?’ Farrar-Drumm turned his back rudely on Fettleworth and cupped a hand round an ear. He rose from his seat and went to the window. ‘Man on a horse,’ he said.

‘Pathan?’

‘No. Scots – wearing trews. A mounted runner, no doubt, but God knows where from, I don’t.’ Farrar-Drumm leaned farther from the window and called out to the rider, who had outflanked Fettleworth’s encampment on the other side of the railway line: ‘I say! That man there, that rider! Who are yer?’

‘I might well ask you the same question, sir.’

‘Might yer indeed. I am General Farrar-Drumm, commanding—’

‘I am Major Lord Brora, second-in-command of the 114th Highlanders.’

‘Ah! And yer regiment?’

‘I have just now informed you, sir.’

‘I mean *where is* yer regiment?’

‘Some thirty miles to the south-west of here, sir, engaged upon disinfestation of the countryside to General Fettleworth’s orders.’ Brora looked tired, and was; he had had a long ride, having mistaken his route and having had to come back upon his tracks. He rode closer and saluted the General. ‘I am surprised to find you here, sir. I have come to take a report from

Captain Ogilvie of my regiment. Where is Captain Ogilvie, may I ask?'

'Can't say,' Farrar-Drumm answered, rasping at his throat.

'I see. Perhaps you'll kindly have him informed that his Major is here, and wishes words with him.'

Farrar-Drumm said irritably. 'He's not damn well here, Major.'

'Really! Why not, sir, pray?' Brora's voice was tart.

'Don't yer take that tone with me, Major,' Farrar-Drumm said. 'I remember yer – we met some time ago in Ootacamund. I didn't like yer then, and I don't like yer now.'

'I'm sorry to hear it, sir. But I have a right to know the whereabouts of my company commanders, and—'

'Not yours, yer Colonel's.' Farrar-Drumm turned away from the window while Brora fumed. A few moments later Farrar-Drumm was replaced by the face of General Fettleworth. Brora saluted again.

Fettleworth said, 'Captain Ogilvie took his company to the west, Major. That, I gather, was a couple or so days ago. No word's been sent back since. I can add only that he was known to have intended entering Chapra. I suggest you ride on and seek your information from the British Resident.'

'Thank you, sir, but I'm more concerned with my niece and sister-in-law than with

Captain Ogilvie—'

'Why didn't you say so, then instead of wasting my time and General Farrar-Drumm's? So far as I'm aware, your niece ... who is your niece?'

'Miss Elliott, sir, and her mother is Lady Mary Elliott – my sister-in-law. Is all well with them and with the train?'

'So far as I'm aware, yes,' Fettleworth answered. 'I've only arrived here from Patna myself within the last half-hour. However, I'm glad you've come, Brora, very glad. Have my mounted runners yet reached your battalion?'

'No runners had reported up to the time I detached, sir.'

Fettleworth snorted. 'Didn't think they blasted well would have! Don't know what things are coming to. Communications are the very devil in India, the very devil! First thing I did when I got here was to send sappers to look for a break in the damn telegraph line, and if they manage to find and repair it, the native buggers'll only go and cut it again – in the pay of the damn Pathans I don't doubt. However, as I was going to say, you can take the message yourself and the sooner you ride back the better. Tell your Colonel this: he's to watch out for a large body of Pathans carrying gold bullion stolen from this train – damn brigands who have set the whole of the north by the ears and who may make a dash for it into your regiment's arms for all I know. Lord Dornoch's to be warned of this.' Fettleworth gave a gesture of dismissal and turned away from the window. Brora opened his mouth, then closed it with an angry snap. He disliked being treated as a messenger, but to argue with either Fettleworth or Farrar-Drumm had always been a pointless exercise.

He rode down the railway line, seeking out his womenfolk.

In Dassar, the night had passed with a sense of anticlimax: the Pathans had attempted an attack but had been beaten back by heavy fire. Thereafter, they had remained beyond the perimeter, laying siege to the remnants of the village and its British holders. An hour or so before the dawn, there had been sounds of more horsemen coming up, riding fast, and the Scots had tensed for another attack, but this attack had not come. Instead, the horsemen had stopped, and there was silence again.

'Someone's brought them a message,' Blaise-Willoughby said in a low voice. They all listened intently for any sound that might give warning of the Pathans riding in; Ogilvie had a sinking feeling that the tribesmen would wear them down by a process of sheer attrition. His Scots couldn't hold on for ever without reinforcements.

After a while they heard the movement of horses, the creak of leather fitments, the rattle of the bayoneted *jezails*. Then more silence as the sounds receded.

'The buggers have moved out,' Blaise-Willoughby said in some astonishment. This was confirmed within the minute by Colour-Sergeant MacTrease.

Ogilvie asked, 'Do you know which way they went, Colour?'

'Not for certain, sir. It's still too dark ... but I've a feeling it was easterly.'

'Easterly! That's strange, isn't it, Major?'

Blaise-Willoughby shrugged; there was a chattering noise from his monkey as the movement shifted it. 'It needn't be. Those messengers ... they could have brought word of some advance from Nowshera or thereabouts. I don't mean there's been any response to Pollinger's message to Nowshera – much too soon, even if he's managed to get through at all, the damn telegraph lines being what they are. But the thing is, I've been out of touch with events in the wider world the last few days, Ogilvie. It's perfectly possible some large-scale troop movements were ordered earlier, and the Pathans have got wind of them and they're buggering off in what appears a safe direction for the time being. But I can't be sure.'

'It makes sense,' Ogilvie said.

'Thanks,' Blaise-Willoughby said drily. 'If I'm right, Dassar won't be bothered any more – not till the Pathans are chased the other way, anyhow!'

'By which time we'll be gone.'

'Perhaps.'

'Why perhaps, Major? I don't intend to hang around here now—'

'Not so fast,' the Political Officer interrupted. 'Suppose the Pathans have left the loot behind, all nicely buried away, all ready for them to pick up at their leisure later on, maybe a lot later on when the dust has settled? Worth a look – don't you think?' Blaise-Willoughby added, 'That young lad I questioned – he could be persuaded to talk again—'

'Too late, Major. He's dead.'

'Oh? Damn!' Blaise-Willoughby looked angry. 'That's unfortunate, I must say.'

'A hunt for buried treasure ... it'd take much too long and it's only a theory in any case. I'm for forced-marching back towards Bundarbar, frankly.'

'To do what?'

'What I was marching back to do when we found Harlow – defend the train. If the Pathans are going back that way, the passengers could be in danger again.'

Blaise-Willoughby said irritably, 'There's nothing to take them back to the train, Ogilvie. In fact they'd be bloody stupid to go back – and the Pathans aren't stupid whatever else they may be.'

'But they're devilish wily, as you well know.'

Blaise-Willoughby gave a sigh. '*Now* what's forming in your wretched military head, Ogilvie?'

'I'm not sure yet. It's just that I don't see the train escaping someone's attentions, even if it's not the Pathans. It's wide open to attack and there are plenty of ordinary bandits around. There's just my RSM and a handful of men to defend it—'

'Fettleworth may have sent reinforcements by now.'

'We can't be sure of that. If he has, well and good. If he hasn't ... do you know, Major, one thing is bothering me and it's this: the Pathans could re-take the train and use the passengers as hostages for the safe conduct of the gold out of India—'

'Bunkum!' Blaise-Willoughby said jeeringly. 'Damn it all, man, the bloody tribes know very well the Raj never gives in to blackmail!'

'I'm not so sure,' Ogilvie said. He sounded obstinate. 'There are plenty of women and children aboard that train, and it would look bad at home – gold bullion before women and children. The Pathans have savvy enough to appreciate that. And we're going to be worse than useless if we sit around in

Dassar – or start digging for gold in the hills!'

'But if we *find* the gold, that cuts the ground from under the Pathans. It could be a better way of protecting your hypothetical hostages, Ogilvie!'

The dawn came up; another day with a promise of good weather, free once more of the teeming rain. The vultures were there, a black cloud settled with the ravening beaks on the fresh Pathan bodies. Ogilvie turned away from the sight, looked around for Colour-Sergeant MacTrease. During the hour before the dawn, a compromise was reached with Blaise-Willoughby: he and Harlow would make their own way into the hills and look for the gold. Ogilvie would detach four privates under a lance-corporal to act as guard and escort; the rest of B Company, or what was left alive, would march out for Bundarbar.

Twelve

'James,' Fiona Elliott said firmly, 'behaved perfectly, Uncle David.'

Brora glowered. 'What does perfectly mean, may I ask?'

'What it says.' Fiona faced him boldly; a snap had come into her voice. 'As an officer and a gentleman, if you want chapter and verse.'

'Damned young puppy!'

Lady Mary took him up on that. 'I don't know why you're so against him, David. He's one of your own regiment, he comes from an *excellent* family and is quite obviously going to go a long way in the army—'

'The farther the better – from me, I mean. I just happen to dislike the sons of Army Commanders who think they can get *daddy* to pull their chestnuts out of the fire for them.'

'Well, that's not true in James' case, David, and I don't care what you say. Just because he bested you twice—'

'That's enough, Mary—'

'When you tried to have him Court

Martialled on some trumped up charge – oh, I've heard all about *that*—'

'Hold your tongue!' Brora shouted, his face livid and his voice thickening as though he were drunk. Almost involuntarily he lifted his right arm, and with it his riding-crop. 'Another god-damn word and I'll thrash the pair of you for blasted scurrilous bitches!'

Lady Mary's hand flew to her mouth, her eyes showing sudden fear. Fiona stood her ground calmly, facing Brora. Along the coach two women screamed and made their way to the exit. Up behind Lord Brora came Mr Wilberforce, bustling and self-important.

'My dear sir, is this necessary? I must protest most strongly—'

Brora swung round. 'Must you indeed! Who the devil are you, sir?'

'My name's Wilberforce, Public Works in—'

'You can stuff your Public Works up your private parts, Mr Wilberforce, for all I care about you. How dare you speak like that to a military officer?' Brora brandished the riding-crop again.

'I merely—'

'You damn Civilians are all the same. Pansies, pimps, parasites – lounge lizards! Damn useless. Get out of my sight immediately or I shall have General Fettleworth clap you in irons.'

'I—'

'Do as I say!' Brora took a pace forward. Wilberforce gaped. Brora seized him, twirled him round, hoisted him in the air by the seat of his pants and the scruff of his neck, and carried him at the run to the exit, whence he pushed him through and let go. Wilberforce collapsed in a moaning heap on the railway line. Brora strode back up the coach, laughing like a hyena, loudly, boisterously, a gleam of satisfaction in his eye. 'That's what they all need – the bums' rush!' he said in a hectoring tone. 'By God, that's done me good! I feel better! I shall spare your hide, sister-in-law, but remember this: you'll cross me again in regard to Captain Ogilvie at your peril, the pair of you!'

Brora turned away along the coach once more, and dropped down to the track. Wilberforce had gathered himself to his feet and was walking stiffly away; faces looked in disdain at Brora from all along the train and from the track where the passengers were taking exercise. Word of the fracas had spread at lightning speed. Marching past, the Regimental Sergeant-Major gave Lord Brora a formal salute, his face expressionless.

'Ha! You there – Cunningham.'

Cunningham halted and marched smartly back. He saluted again. 'Sir!'

'Why are you skulking at the train, Cunningham? Why are you not with Captain Ogilvie?'

Cunningham's face was a picture. 'I am not skulking, sir. I have never skulked in my life, sir. I was *ordered* to remain behind by Captain Ogilvie, sir.'

'I see. To defend the train, I suppose?'

'Aye, sir, to defend it.'

'As you did when you and Captain Ogilvie allowed the damn Pathans to make off with the bullion? Well, your role's over now General Fettleworth has arrived to conduct a *competent* defence. You'll rejoin the battalion with me when I ride back.'

'With much respect, sir, I am under orders—'

'From Captain Ogilvie! My orders are superior to his, Cunningham, and you'll do as you're told – by me. I trust you understand?'

'I do, sir—'

'Good! And in the meantime, adjust the set of your sporran. I'll not have a bad example set before the rest of the division. That's all. You may carry on.'

Brora strode away, turning his back on the Regimental Sergeant-Major's salute. Cunningham's thoughts were lurid; he was shaking with anger. To speak to an RSM like that at any time, let alone before other ranks, natives and Civilians ... it was atrocious behaviour, unforgiveable. Officers normally accorded a Sergeant-Major the 'mister', too. The Major was a bastard, no doubt of that, and impossible to serve under. It was always said that there was no bastard like a gently born bastard, and Lord Brora was the living proof of that. The man was out of his time, might have been acceptable in the days of Blenheim, of Waterloo, even of Balaclava when a Sergeant-Major could be stripped of his rank at the whim of men like Brora, and then flogged as a private soldier. Those days were gone, and bad cess to them, Cunningham thought, seething as he marched away.

Early that afternoon, as Ogilvie with his depleted company was not far off half-way to Chapra from the village of Dassar, Bloody Francis passed the order for the First Division to move out from Bundarbar in continuation of its westward thrust. Lakenham had demurred, pointing out that the train would once again be undefended, but Fettleworth rejected this.

'Pooh! It'll not be attacked, Lakenham, why should it be? It didn't come under attack again before my arrival, and it won't after my departure. But I tell you what I'll do: any of the Civilians who wish it can be ferried back in the boats to Patna, and thence—'

'On dry land, sir?'

'What?'

'The floods have subsided.'

'You *always* dredge up the difficulties, Lakenham.'

So the orders were to stand; Fettleworth, when his Chief of Staff had reported the division ready, remounted his steed and took his leave of General Farrar-Drumm, who descended from his command coach to announce that he still intended to remain and not ride out to join Southern Army, always assuming he could have found them now that they had been sent beyond his ken.

'I shall not desert the train, General.'

'Quite, quite.' In point of fact, Fettleworth had omitted to consider what might best be done with Farrar-Drumm. 'I understand, General. I wish you good luck.'

'I wish yer the same,' Farrar-Drumm said in an aggrieved tone; it had long rankled, and now rankled more than ever, that he had not been accorded the extra accolade of a lieutenant-general. It was far from just; he was a good deal older than Fettleworth and if his command was in truth not as important as that of Sir Iain Ogilvie's Northern Army at Murree, he was an experienced campaigner and that ought to count for something. However, there it was; and he still would not salute Fettleworth, so the curious pantomime of the ready but silent buglers was once again presented as the

First Division ground slowly away, slipping and sliding in the abominable mud left behind by the floods' retreat.

Lord Brora watched the departure, a cynical look upon his face. He had an idea that Fettleworth, once he had given his orders that Brora was to ride his message to the Royal Strathspey, had forgotten his existence. Well, so be it! Brora's lip curled. As a major in a Highland regiment, as an earl as belted as Lord Dornoch, he was not a damned runner and his presence was needed to back up the train's defence if an attack should come. One senile major-general, one warrant officer and a few privates! An active officer was much needed as stiffening.

He said as much to Farrar-Drumm when that officer queried his presence. Farrar-Drumm said hoarsely, 'Well, I dare say you're right, Major. I should have someone to stand between me and the rank and file, I suppose, though I'm perfectly satisfied with that sar'nt-major from yer own regiment. First-class feller, doncher know.'

'I find him uppish.'

'I find yer rude.' Farrar-Drumm turned his back.

Blaise-Willoughby and the Political Officer from Chapra made their way on foot into the hills lying to the north of Dassar; it was a wearying walk that was due to end in a stiffish climb, and both men were soon drenched with sticky sweat. Blaise-Willoughby loosened his collar and tie, cursing the fuggy atmosphere. 'One thing we haven't got,' he observed, 'is a spade.'

'I doubt if they'll have buried the gold, Major. It'll be behind some rock, or possibly in a cave.'

'Yes, perhaps.'

They plodded on; Blaise-Willoughby's feet were already making him wonder if he had embarked on a wild goose chase and he half wished he had gone with Ogilvie. At least he would have been given some sort of animal to ride once he reached Chapra. As it was, the hills were a devilish long way and would take a lot of walking around once they were reached, and after that he would have to walk to Chapra, a daunting prospect. Harlow was a younger man, able to take it better.

'Don't walk so damn fast,' Blaise-Willoughby said.

'Sorry.' Harlow slowed a little.

'I can't keep it up, not that pace. Walking is a hobby of mine – or was – but not at forced-march pace.' Blaise-Willoughby looked round at the guard and escort, marching in rear. Soon the climb began, gentle at first, then the angle increased. Blaise-Willoughby called a halt and they all sat on the ground, with one of the escorting soldiers being sent by his lance-corporal to act as a picquet on some higher ground. Blaise-Willoughby lit his pipe and enjoyed the aroma as the blue smoke rose, though Wolseley chattered away on his shoulder, having never become really accustomed to the sight and smell of Master burning.

Blaise-Willoughby's smoke was interrupted by the sudden fast descent of the posted picquet, who made a report as soon as he was in earshot: 'Corporal, I got a quick sight of a Pathan, away to the west!'

The lance-corporal approached Blaise-Willoughby, who said, 'All right, Corporal, I heard that. Was your picquet seen?'

'I can't say, sir,' the private answered, 'but I think I would have been.'

'So do I,' Blaise-Willoughby said. He knocked out his pipe, then rubbed his jaw reflectively. 'It begins to look as though we may be getting warm, don't you think, Corporal?'

'The native was on guard, you mean, sir?'

'Yes.' Blaise-Willoughby got to his feet. 'I'm going to assume we've been spotted via your picquet and that there's nothing to be lost by going on openly. Except our lives, perhaps! Full alertness now, Corporal.'

'Aye, sir.'

'All rifles ready to open as soon as I give the word.' By this time Blaise-Willoughby and Harlow had both drawn their revolvers. No time was lost now; the party made their way higher, all eyes watching the crests of the hills for the briefly-shown turban or the long snout of the *jezail* that would give the warning. So far, the heights stayed clear. On reaching the crest, the soldier who had acted as picquet took the lead at Blaise-Willoughby's order.

He said, 'I'm not too sure just where it was, sir—'

'Just do your best, laddie. The general direction will help, and the first bullet will give us the exact spot.'

Amid a good deal of tension now, the party advanced with rounds up the spouts of the Lee Enfields. If their luck was out, one of them was going to get that first bullet; none of them had any doubts about that. Sweat poured from them all; Harlow was shaking a little and Blaise-Willoughby, giving him a shrewd glance, asked, 'Your first time in this sort of action, isn't it, Roger?'

Harlow nodded.

'You've faced the back alleys. They're worse in my opinion – *much* worse!'

The younger man gave a grin. 'I'm more used to them, Major.'

Blaise-Willoughby understood. There were many times, and this was one of them, when he was very glad of his army years.

Harlow was a direct recruit to the Political Service, with no benefit of drill and discipline, in background a Civilian. Blaise-Willoughby, in his infantry days, had done any amount of patrols and had come under fire many times as well. Not that that ever reduced the prickle in the spine, the feeling of the hair rising at the back of the neck, or the queasiness in the stomach when you knew that the hidden enemy had you ready in his gun-sights. Such was part and parcel of service in the Indian field ... and even the vultures seemed to know, with their uncanny instinct, that men were about to die. They knew now: they were wheeling overhead, keeping their height for the time being but handy to swoop in when the meal was ready. Blaise-Willoughby shook a fist in the air, and muttered curses; like all who served in India, he detested the birds of prey.

As the fist was shaken, the first bullet came. A puff of smoke was seen behind a craggy rock to the left and a little ahead of the advancing party. A man spun, hit in the shoulder, but didn't fall.

Blaise-Willoughby shouted, 'Take cover – there!' He pointed to an overhang on their left. Before they had all made it, the *jezail* opened again. The bullet hit rock and ricochetted away harmlessly. Then they were in cover.

'What now, sir?' the lance-corporal asked.

'We wait a while to see if an attack is mounted. If it isn't, we go in fast for where the smoke puffs came from.'

'They'll likely shift position, sir.'

'Very likely,' Blaise-Willoughby said, 'but we'll have to chance that. I don't propose being pinned down here indefinitely, Corporal!'

'No, sir.' Lance-Corporal Finlay answered cheerfully enough; he was ambitious, and meant one day to make Regimental Sergeant-Major. But he was young, one of a fairly recent replacement from the regimental depot at Invermore in Scotland, sent out in the room of those killed whilst on patrol from Peshawar; and he was having a bad attack of nerves that showed in the whiteness of his knuckles as he gripped his rifle. The vultures were hovering still, and he wished desperately that they would go away. They did; they rose higher in a flurry of black feathers and predatory beaks as the hidden *jezail* opened once more and a bullet scraped across the rocky overhang, bringing down chips and debris. But the vultures came back again all too soon.

The men waited for events to decide their course of action. Blaise-Willoughby yawned and lit up his pipe again, glad enough of another rest. Harlow pulled out a handkerchief and wiped the sweat from his forehead; his native clothing stank in his own nostrils. Lance-Corporal Finlay, very regimental, displayed his nerves again when he reprimanded a private for taking off his helmet without orders.

'Sorry, Coporal.' The helmet went back on.

Blaise-Willoughby frowned. If he was smoking, a private could remove his headgear if he wished, but discipline was discipline and he didn't interfere. In any case, he understood; his army days were coming back now – this was the first time he'd indulged in field action in command of men since he'd been seconded to the Political Service, and, much as he had disparaged the military mind in the years between, he knew now that he still possessed some vestiges of it himself.

The wait went on and nothing happened: no attack, and no more firing. After a full hour had passed since the last shot, Blaise-Willoughby got to his feet.

'We advance,' he said. 'We come out at the double, and we go right for where the *jezails* open from. Each man to fire independently as soon as the Pathans open. Ready, Corporal Finlay?'

'Aye, sir.' Sweat flowed freely, running into Finlay's eyes. 'All ready, sir.'

'Good. Watch carefully and act fast. We're going to make it.' Blaise-Willoughby checked the chambers of his revolver, then pulled down his white jacket, straightening some of the fearful rumples: the army was back with a vengeance. Then he said, 'Right! We go – *now*.'

He led the dash out. The firing started the moment he showed himself. The number of *jezails* was uncertain, but Blaise-Willoughby fancied there were three or four. The bullets zipped down, and the man with the wounded shoulder was hit again, this time in the throat. He went down choking; and had to be left where he fell until the action was over. The rest pounded on desperately, climbing towards the crest above as the *jezails*, reloaded now, opened again. The Scots were firing back as they climbed; above them a native rose in the air, screaming, blood pouring from his chest, and then fell, bouncing off the rocky hillside as he went, to land in a bloody heap below the steadily advancing party. The remaining *jezails* kept up the fire, and the next to die was Harlow, who spun down to join the Pathan below. Blaise-Willoughby, concentrating ahead, was as yet unaware that Harlow had gone. Reaching the crest with Finlay at his side and the three remaining privates coming up in rear, he faced the *jezails* and the rusty bayonets man to man. He fired rapid rounds from his revolver and another Pathan fell with blood gushing from his mouth. Then a bullet smashed the revolver from Blaise-Willoughby's hand, and badly wounded the hand itself: two fingers went. From beside him Finlay fired back: another Pathan died instantly. Then the last of them came in with the bayonet, and as a Scots private took the point of the blade in his stomach, another *jezail* opened from the rear. Blaise-Willoughby was down on the ground, trying to recover his revolver in the hope that it might yet work and could be fired, with shaky aim, by his left hand, when Lance-Corporal Finlay staggered and fell, his face deathly white, and collapsed in a heap at Blaise-Willoughby's side. The Political Officer seized his rifle, took aim, holding the weapon to his left shoulder, teeth gritted against the searing agony of his right hand, and fired as rapidly as he was able.

Thirteen

By late afternoon, Ogilvie's company passed to the south of Chapra; Bundarbar lay now within a day's march. Ogilvie expected to reach the train by the next dawn. Before the daylight faded he called a halt and supper was prepared by the field kitchen, a frugal meal of soup and stale bread and corned beef, washed down with the contents of the water-bottles. The company relaxed for a brief spell under the care of the picquets and then were ordered to their feet, to fall in and march on through the night. By this time spoor had been picked up, an indication in the muddy ground that horsemen had passed by, many horsemen riding in the direction of Bundarbar; and Ogilvie believed that his guess had been a good one, that the gold-thieving Pathans were making for the train.

He was right.

A matter of some hours before, the Pathans, riding east, had also passed to the South of Chapra; a little farther on they had deviated north when their outriders, posted ahead as scouts, had seen in the distance the van of a great army on the march westwards. The Pathans had ridden out of sight and had then dismounted and lain low until Bloody Francis Fettleworth had passed on in all ignorance, making for he knew not where but hoping to find his quarry on the way. As that quarry laughed up its sleeve at the passing soldiers of the Raj, and then rode on towards Bundarbar, General Fettleworth complained about the total lack of natives who, had they manifested themselves, might usefully have been questioned. The absence of such, Lakenham suggested, was no doubt due to the floods.

'I don't see why. The floods have gone.'

'And left many dead behind, sir.'

'One is very aware of that, Lakenham, but where are the living? One would have thought they'd return.'

'To what?' Lakenham asked, waving a hand around the horizons. 'To utter devastation, to huts that are no longer there because they have floated away, to lands whose very earth has moved and their crops and livestock with it? No doubt they'll come back in time, and try to start life afresh. But not just yet.'

'Frightened of the disease, d'you suppose?'

'Perhaps, sir. Perhaps that is it.' Lakenham's words had, he hoped, a sound of finality. Argument with Bloody Francis always led round in a circle and Lakenham found the experience highly frustrating. The First Division moved on; a few natives were indeed found as the day progressed, sad men and women rootling through the remains of their village to find what might be salvaged, or to look for the bodies of their dead. These men and women were questioned, but without result. The hopeless look in their eyes was guarantee enough that they would not have been occupying their thoughts with any stray Pathans who might have crossed their paths. Bloody Francis, surveying their plight from horseback, cleared his throat gruffly and fumbled in the pockets of his tunic. He cast down a handful of rupees, and the flood survivors scrabbled for them on the muddy ground, uttering benisons on the mighty Raj. Bloody Francis moved away.

'Poor beggars,' he said. 'Her Majesty would be proud.'

'Of what, sir?'

'They're loyal yet, Lakenham – loyal yet!'

Darkness fell around the silent train; one more night in the care of the few soldiers of the Royal Strathspey, now added to by the presence of their Major. As that darkness came down, Lord Brora walked the deserted railway station alongside the coaches where the Civilians were already bedding down for the night, uncomfortably, on the seats. Carrying a guard lantern, he opened the door of the stationmaster's office and went in; the body of the stationmaster, he had been told by Cunningham, had been burned in the engine's furnace along with the other dead.

The room had an oppressive feel, something that made even Brora's hair rise though he knew not why. He gave himself a shake, moved across to the telegraph and, for the tenth time since his arrival, tried to activate it. It was dead still, as dead as the stationmaster himself. The stationmaster's gold-braided cap hung from a hook, no doubt put back there after the removal of his body. Brora grinned tightly to himself: for a certainty a damn chi-chi would have put his uniform cap on his head before going out to meet the Pathans, confronting them with the emblem of the British Raj atop his semi-dusky skin! That, however, hadn't saved him; he had probably died a more painful death because of the colour of his skin and his loyalty to the British, whose half-blood flowed in his veins. Brora looked at other things in that sad office: the stationmaster had been something of a family man. There were silver-framed photographs of what seemed to be the man's mother and father and of his brothers and sisters, five of them in an off-white group of varying ages, some darker than the others. The mother had been a Hindu woman of some beauty, and very dark-skinned. The father was depicted in the uniform of a battery sergeant-major of the field gunners, moustachioed and martial, with a fierce expression. Damn fool, Brora thought, why the devil couldn't he have found some decent housemaid when in England, instead of fathering a race of stationmasters and train drivers out here in India? The chi-chis were a problem not of their own making but of the making of their fathers, serving soldiers to a man who had not been able to confine their off-duty pleasures to the proper ones of beer and brothels. Better if they'd all been castrated.

Lord Brora, looking at the photographs and concentrating on his own ponderings, and hearing nothing to disturb him, was taken utterly unawares when he felt the prick of a sharp knife through his uniform jacket.

A voice in his ear said softly, 'Do not move, Major sahib. Do not cry out, or you die instantly.'

'Who are you?' Brora asked, harshly.

The knife went in a shade deeper and Brora felt the run of blood down his backbone. 'Softer, Major Sahib. The lantern – extinguish it at once. The knife is ready.'

Sweat poured down Brora's face. Once he got out of this, the damn picquets would face Court Martial, so would Cunningham. But in the meantime he had no option other than to reach forward and extinguish the guard lantern which he had set on the stationmaster's desk. This he did, and a moment later, although he had still heard no sound at all, he felt the presence of other natives around him. Hands were laid on him, the knife remained in place, and some filthy material was placed over his mouth, nose and eyes and drawn tight behind his head. Then he was lifted off his feet and borne away into the darkness.

'Is the train secure for the night, Sar'nt-Major?' Farrar-Drumm asked.

'So far as possible, sir. I have few men, sir.'

Farrar-Drumm gave a sage nod. 'Yes, yes, I understand yer difficulties, Sar'nt-Major. None better. I remember in the Zulu War ... I was advancing on Ulundi with a handful of men – Welshmen, as a matter of fact, stout fellows – against many hundreds of Zulu warriors with spears and so on, and shields, and tufts on their legs.' He broke off to cough, a lengthy business and a distressing one that left him gasping like a landed fish. 'What was I saying, Sar'nt-Major?'

'The Zulu War, sir. Many hundreds of Zulus, against a few Welshmen. May I ask what happened, sir?'

'What happened?' Farrar-Drumm asked, sounding astonished.

'Aye, sir—'

'Fancy asking such a question! We beat 'em off, of course.' Farrar-Drumm was quite put about, and was intending to utter further strictures when Cunningham interrupted without ceremony.

'Begging your pardon, sir, something's up—'

'*What's* up?'

'The Major, sir. His lantern's gone out suddenly. I must find out why.'

Cunningham, who had been glancing out of the window towards the stationmaster's office, left the General's presence without further delay, leaving Farrar-Drumm to click his tongue in some annoyance. The British Army was falling upon evil days indeed when even sergeant-majors could dismiss themselves from a General's presence without so much as by-your-leave. Damn disgrace, really! General Farrar-Drumm coughed again, and wheezed alarmingly. Of course, Cunningham was perfectly right to do his duty if he found some alarm, which frankly Farrar-Drumm did not, in the sudden extinguishing of Lord Brora's light. If Brora himself could be extinguished, Farrar-Drumm would be better pleased; Lord Brora had spent a good deal of that very day lecturing him on tactics and strategy in the modern world, just as though he needed bringing up to date. Farrar-Drumm had been immensely angry, not only on account of the great difference in their relative ranks, but also because it was so much better to disregard the modern world and to inhabit the old, when men had been men and a handful of Welshmen could rout hundreds of blasted Zulus, the kind of thing that didn't seem to happen any more. Farrar-Drumm had shown his anger in the end, after trying to be polite to a very rude man, and Brora had left him, but not before a loud mutter about old fools with one-and-a-half feet in the grave. However, the wretched fellow's light had gone out, and if Cunningham saw trouble in that, then, again, he was right to do something about it. Perhaps it *did* spell trouble. Sir Clarence Farrar-Drumm rose to his feet and called for Captain Smyth to help him remain there.

It was as he stood perfecting his balance that the trouble came. Shadows suddenly materialised from the darkness of the railway track, very solid shadows that rushed aboard the train. Pathans bearing *jezails* and bayonets, desperate-looking men with filthy, smelly garments and turbans and bearded faces. Hundreds of them ... history was repeating itself, with the difference that this time the defence was to be Scots rather than Welsh. The Pathans were just as sadistic a foe as the Zulus, who had had few standards, despite being ruled by a king.

As the Pathans crowded aboard his coach, General Farrar-Drumm hooked his thumbs into his Sam Browne belt and stared towards them. *'Imshi!'* he said. *'Jaldee!'* He felt that perhaps he had got it wrong; they took no notice, but crowded towards him. 'You tell them, Smyth.'

'I – I think it's a waste of time, sir.'

'Oh, nonsense, Smyth, they just need firm handling, that's all.' The memories of Ulundi crowded thick and fast, like the Pathans themselves, and Farrar-Drumm drew his revolver from its holster and flourished it. 'Back, you devils!' he roared out. 'Back, back, I say!' Then an attack of coughing silenced him, and a bullet from a *jezail*, sounding like thunder in the enclosed space and accompanied by an appalling stench of gunpowder, took the revolver from his fingers, which thereafter felt numb and sore. Blood dripped down. One of the Pathans approached, grinning.

'Do not be foolish again, old General sahib. You will not be hurt. We, who come from Afghanistan and are good Muslims, respect our grand-parents and our great-grandparents. Those whose hair is white and whose bodies are frail are treated kindly.'

Farrar-Drumm gave an angry wheeze, but was past speech for the time being.

Farther along Farrar-Drumm's coach, the Regimental Sergeant-Major was also under guard of the Pathans, having been captured on his way to seek Brora. Three *jezails* covered him. So far, the attack had been bloodless, apart from General Farrar-Drumm's fingers. The small party of Scots had been overwhelmed in the sudden rush from the darkness, and there had been no chance to offer any resistance at all.

Cunningham asked, 'What do you intend to do?' He asked this in English; one of the Pathans answered him, also in English.

'We intend to go back to Afghanistan.'

'Then I think you're going the wrong way, are you not?'

'You do not understand. We shall not leave British India without the gold.'

'Ah, so that's it! It's been recovered from you?'

The head was shaken; Cunningham could almost fancy he saw the lice being thrown clear of the turban and the greasy matted hair. 'It has not, Sergeant-Major sahib. It is with us still, but the soldiers of the Raj are pressing us, and it has become impossible to take the gold across the frontier into Afghanistan, so—'

'So you're taking the train and its passengers hostage – is that so?'

'Yes, that is indeed so, Sergeant-Major sahib. They are to be the safe conduct for the gold. When advice reaches us that the gold is beyond the frontier of India, then the people will be released.'

Knowing what the answer would be. Cunningham nevertheless asked the question: 'And when you're attacked, which you will be since you'll need to announce what you've done? What then?'

'Any attack leads to the immediate death of everyone aboard the train, Sergeant-Major sahib. We bring explosives, and the train will be blown to pieces if necessary.'

'And your announcement? How do you make that? Bundarbar station is out of communication—'

The man interrupted with a grin. 'Yes. For not much longer. When our local friends and allies against the Raj have repaired the line where they cut it for the second time – after the General sahib had sent soldiers to mend it – then communication with Patna will return, and Patna will communicate with Calcutta and the great and mighty Viceroy of the Queen-Empress.'

'Yes, I see. I have the feeling you'll get a dusty answer, my friend! In the meantime, perhaps you'll tell me what you've done with my Major?'

'Your Major sahib is safe. Sergeant-Major

sahib, and will remain so if he does what we wish.'

Cunningham gave a sardonic smile. Lord Brora was a bastard right enough, but he wasn't the kind of bastard who gave help to the enemy, as the enemy would find out. In the meantime the enemy didn't like British captives who smiled at them in a superior fashion, and for his pains Cunningham got a smash in the kidneys from the butt of one of the *jezails*.

Lord Brora, in a foul temper and half asphyxiated by the clinging material and its revolting smell, had his covering removed once he had arrived at his destination. He had no idea where this destination was; the only clues were dampness and the sound of water washing close past one wall of the place where he had been taken. He made the assumption that he was alongside a river, the river that flowed through Bundarbar – the wide and holy Ganges itself, though presumably not at all holy to his captors, the Muslim Pathans. Brora was thrown to the floor on his arrival. The floor was hard but wet, with a slop of water seeping through from the river wall as he took it to be. He had a feeling he was below ground and river level. He stared up into the muzzles of a number of *jezails*, and when he tried to get to his feet he was pushed down again by the bayonets and then one of the Pathans stepped forward and seized an arm which he tied with rope to a ringbolt set in the wall away from the river; at the same time another man secured the other arm, after which they turned their attentions to the legs and Brora sat spreadeagled and helpless, uttering threats.

'You'll swing for this, outside the civil jail—'

'We shall not, Major sahib. Before that happens to us, you will be dead. You will not wish to die.'

'I don't give a fig. I'm a soldier, not some damn pimp who—'

The butt of a *jezail*, aimed for the kidneys as in the case of the RSM, stopped Brora for the moment. 'You will die, if die you must, by terrible means,' he was told. The means were not gone into. 'As a major sahib of the British Raj, you will be of importance—'

'You're damn right! I am! You'll never get away with this – kidnapping *me* like this! Do you know who I am? I am Major the Earl of Brora, a peer of the British realm, of Her Majesty the Queen-Empress, second-in-command of the 114th Highlanders, the Queen's Own Royal Strathspey. I am not some common greengrocer's boy from Peckham who's managed to jump himself up to a commission. And I think you're going to find you've made one damn big mistake!'

The man shook his head. 'Not so. There is far from a mistake, if you are so important!' The voice sounded exultant, not in the least apologetic. 'No, there is not a mistake, Major sahib, earl sahib of many distinctions. You will be useful to us, but for now we shall not tell you how this will be so. Instead, you will be left to ponder on how terrible is your present situation, and that of the persons in the train at the station.'

'You'll not be hurting them?'

There was a shrug. 'Perhaps, perhaps not.'

'You are a black devil, a bastard, a damn *native*—'

A *jezail* butt slammed into Brora's forehead and he slumped in his ropes with blood pouring. He was unconscious when the men went away, slamming, locking and bolting the door behind them after tying a filthy gag firmly across Brora's mouth.

Early next morning, the Pathans' communication from Bundarbar reached Government House in Calcutta via Patna; and set the whole of the Viceregal staff by the ears. Sir George White, Commander-in-Chief, was summoned by Colonel Durand, the Military Secretary, to attend upon His Excellency. Lord Elgin, Viceroy of India, handed a transcript of the message to White. Having read, Sir George looked up. He said,

'We can't concede. Can't possibly!'

'If we don't, the effect's going to be bad.'

'Where?'

Elgin, who understood what White was getting at, said abruptly. 'At home.'

'Bugger home. We're in India, Your Excellency.'

'I need no reminding of that, Sir George.'

White nodded. 'No, indeed. I'm sorry – I apologise. But you'll realise what would follow from any concessions, Your Excellency. India would break down, disintegrate, with every damned—'

Elgin broke in, gesturing impatiently. 'Oh, come, you exaggerate!'

'I think I do not. The Raj must be strong. That is essential to its survival. One chink in the armour, and the result's catastrophe. The Raj must never give in to blackmail or threat. I repeat the word: never! As Commander-in-Chief in India, sir, I cannot agree to any act of – of appeasement of murderers, kidnappers, lawbreakers of any sort in fact.' Sir George got to his feet, his expression hard. 'The gold must and will be found, Your Excellency, and the train at Bundarbar must and will be relieved. And I propose to give orders to Sir Iain Ogilvie at Murree that not a single Pathan is to cross the North-West Frontier unchallenged, and—'

'A tall order, isn't it?' Elgin said.

White nodded. 'Yes, indeed it is. But I know Ogilvie will carry it out to the best of his ability. It's true the First Division of Northern Army is detached from his command at this moment on account of the flood disaster, but I shall see to it that all officers from Murree on local leave, and all officers detached for courses, re-join immediately. In the meantime there are troopships due in Bombay with regiments from home. Those regiments will be entrained for the Frontier upon disembarkation. In my view, sir, there is no need whatsoever to concede anything to the Pathans.'

Elgin paced the room, backwards and forwards, frowning, deeply disturbed. 'You make much of the frontier, Sir George. I am more concerned about the train's passengers.'

'I am equally concerned,' White said. 'I've already referred to the First Division of Ogilvie's command, sir. The floods are gone from the vicinity of Bundarbar, but General Fettleworth remains in the area. He'll not have marched too far west yet. The First Division is well placed to retake the train and its passengers, and orders will go at once to General Fettleworth to this effect.'

'But carefully,' Elgin said. There was a warning in his voice although his words suggested agreement with the Commander-in-Chief. 'Durand?'

'Sir?'

'Read the relevant part of the Pathans' message again, if you please, Durand.'

The Military Secretary took up the message and read out: 'The first sign of an attack on the train will lead to instant death for the hostages.'

'That is to be well noted, Sir George,' the Viceroy said.

Aboard the train, the atmosphere was growing worse. General Farrar-Drumm wheezed impotently at Captain Smyth, bound with ropes as he was himself and seated next to him. If only he could strike back, and lay about him with his cavalry sabre as he had done in the Crimea and in the Zulu War! General Farrar-Drumm breathed fire but had no current means of using it. He rumbled and coughed alarmingly. He knew precisely the position he was in and to some extent he could predict the response from Calcutta. Like Sir George White, he knew there could be no giving in to the demands of the tribesmen; but he knew also, because the damned Pathans had told him so as if he wasn't experienced enough to guess for himself, that the moment any British force was seen to approach, then the knives and bayonets would be busy on him and everyone else aboard the unfortunate train. Strongly connected to this was a very great worry: the nearest British force was the First Division, with the bulk of his own Southern Army also somewhere in the vicinity. He was not there to command the latter, but General Fettleworth was, and Fettleworth was not a subtle man at all. Fettleworth believed in parades and marches, bands and drums – believed very passionately, so Farrar-Drumm had heard, that the best way to subdue the natives was to send his division out on a show of strength, the infantry marching with fixed bayonets behind the fifes and drums, the cavalry cantering in circles to the strains of "Bonnie Dundee"...

Not, Farrar-Drumm prayed, this time.

Fourteen

Away to the west, in the hills above the village of Dassar, Blaise-Willoughby came slowly round from a state of unconsciousness. He blinked in the light of a high moon that silvered the crests around where he lay; for some while he was confused, wondering where he was and how he had got there. Then by degrees it came back to him: there had been a fight with the Pathans on guard – on guard they must surely have been – on the gold. Blaise-Willoughby's head ached abominably and he felt most extremely sick and his forehead, he found when he lifted a hand towards the ache, was thick with dried blood and there was an enormous lump.

He licked at dry lips, feeling a desperate thirst, and called out shakily for Lance-Corporal Finlay of the Royal Strathspey before recalling that Finlay had been killed and he, Blaise-Willoughby, had taken his rifle and carried on the fight. Faintness overcoming him, Blaise-Willoughby shut his eyes and drifted off eventually into sleep, a refreshing sleep this time. When he awoke again the dawn was in the sky, and he felt quite a lot better though still had that terrible thirst, now indeed increased, and also a ravening hunger. He pulled himself to a sitting position, saw one of the dead Scots' water-bottles, removed it from the body and took a long drink. While he was drinking, he became aware that he was not alone. Behind the rock against which he had propped himself was a vulture, eating a Pathan. Native feet were visible, moving to the beak's peck. The noise and the smell were horrible, utterly revolting. Blaise-Willoughby picked up a chunk of rock and lobbed it over; there was an angry cry and a flap of wings and the dreadful bird rose in the air and hovered over Blaise-Willoughby with bloody human flesh dripping from the end of its beak like a pennant.

Blaise-Willoughby staggered to his feet, felt sick again, but moved doggedly, determined to establish what his position was. This didn't take him very long: he was alone, the sole survivor of the party that had marched from Dassar, and of the Pathan gold-defenders as well. Except for Wolseley his faithful monkey. He found Wolseley crouched miserably in a small recess in the rock, a sort of monkey-sized cavelet, nursing a broken leg and staring from huge, mournful black eyes.

Blaise-Willoughby came close to tears.

'Poor old chap,' he said tenderly. 'Poor old chap...' He felt quite frantic; no vet handy! But he found some branches which he broke up and with the aid of a strip torn from his shirt he fashioned a splint and applied this with immense difficulty to the leg. Whilst doing so, he became aware of something interesting right behind Wolseley's backside: wood – what looked like the corner of a box.

Blaise-Willoughby caught his breath. It couldn't be! Yet the Pathans had been on guard just here, and had fought to the death. There had to be a good reason for that. Blaise-Willoughby, feeling intense excitement but not yet daring to believe what he felt already in his bones, finished the splinting of Wolseley's leg to the accompaniment of much chatter and protest; then with shaking hands he tore and ripped away at the earth. Out came the box: it bore government markings in indication of its contents. Blaise-Willoughby, staring in awe at riches and uttering thanks to the Almighty, tore again at the earth. The burial had been recent and the earth and small rocks came away with comparative ease. And there it all was, box upon box, what was almost certainly the whole consignment intact.

His heart thumping, Blaise-Willoughby sat back on his heels and stared and thought. It was a risk to leave it, of course, but a risk that had to be taken. Blaise-Willoughby knew that somehow or other he had to reach Chapra and it was going to be a devilish long walk for an unwell man with a duck's-egg lump on his forehead.

At about the same time as the word of the Pathans' ultimatum had reached the Viceroy in Calcutta, James Ogilvie and his depleted company, somewhat later than had been hoped, reached the vicinity of Bundarbar. Marching on, Ogilvie came within sight of the railway station. As he did so, he saw two armed Pathans, apparently on guard. Dismayed and anxious, he halted the Scots; Colour-Sergeant MacTrease ran up from the rear and saluted.

'Sir! You've seen—'

'Yes, I have, Colour. No need to ask what's happened!'

'No, sir.'

'The question is—' Ogilvie broke off as MacTrease pointed over his shoulder. Turning, he saw two more Pathans riding towards him, one of them bearing a white flag.

'Flag of truce,' he said. 'Well, at least we'll hear what's going on aboard the train, I suppose!' They all waited in an uneasy silence as the Pathans rode up, and halted a few paces clear of the British troops, and grinned down from their horses.

'You come to attack the train?' the flag-bearer asked. speaking in Pushtu.

'I came not to attack,' Ogilvie answered steadily. returning the man's stare, 'but to defend. It seems I am too late.'

'Yes, too late, Captain sahib.' The man paused. 'You are one of those that wears the skirt, and plays the instrument that squeals like a wounded pig. There is another such aboard the train – a Sergeant-Major sahib, who is yet alive, but who will not remain so if you attack.'

'And the others?'

'They also will die. We are strong in numbers, you are not. To attack would be so foolish!'

'And your terms? What do you want?'

The Pathan smiled; his companion kept his *jezail* aimed full at Ogilvie, and never mind the flag of truce waving beside him. 'Our terms have been sent to the great Viceroy in Calcutta, who by now will perhaps be considering them. His decision will be sent back to us – and only a very foolish Captain sahib would step in before the wishes of his Viceroy are known!'

Ogilvie gave a brief nod; he had taken the point well enough. He said, 'I shall not attack, unless I learn that you have harmed anyone aboard the train.'

'No one will be harmed,' the Pathan said. 'No one – until it is necessary to convince the Raj that we mean what we say and intend to get that for which we have asked. For now, Captain sahib, go in peace.'

Ogilvie passed the order for the Scots to turn about and march away. MacTrease started to protest. 'Retreat, sir? They have the sar'nt-major, sir!'

'I know, and I don't have to say I'm sorry about that, Colour. But I had no option. The best way to help Mr Cunningham, to help them all, is to go carefully. It's certainly not up to a captain of infantry to pre-empt the decisions of His Excellency the Viceroy of India! March out, if you please, Colour.'

'Aye, sir.' MacTrease still looked bitter. 'Where to, sir, for God's sake?'

Ogilvie pointed to the north-west. 'The bridge across the river at Bundarbar village,' he said. 'That's where we'll fall out and bivouac. It overlooks the station and the train, and it's as good a camp as any.'

'Aye, sir, and less bloody muddy,' MacTrease said. He marched away and ordered the about turn, and B Company began to retreat, unwillingly, behind its pipes and drums. The pipes and drums were heard aboard the train; Cunningham heard them and knew they must be from the Royal Strathspey, the only Highland regiment in the vicinity so far as he was aware. Would it be Captain Ogilvie, or would it be Lord Dornoch? He sat in his bonds and fidgeted, sweat pouring down his face. Whoever it was, they were marching away. His thoughts were as bitter, as frustrated as those of MacTrease, but his trust was still, as it would always be, in the regiment. The pipes also penetrated the disturbed mind of Sir Clarence Farrar-Drumm; he didn't like them very much, preferring the sound of a mounted band, tinny though some said mounted bands were. The fools – all those who were not cavalrymen – said that. Farrar-Drumm wheezed away angrily, noting, like Cunningham, that the pipes were fading into the distance.

'Wonder what it's all about, Smyth?' he asked.

'Scots, I believe, sir,' Captain Smyth said helpfully. 'Marching away, sir—'

'Oh, save yer breath, boy, save yer damn breath!'

In another coach, Fiona Elliott, also bound with ropes, sat with Lady Mary and Mr Wilberforce, the latter having contrived to spend his imprisonment with the most socially important persons aboard, relatives of the Earl of Brora, no less, who was an undoubted aristocrat even if a rude and violent one ... Mr Wilberforce had overheard a thing or two indiscreetly uttered by the younger lady, and he understood they had little time for Lord Brora, which was as comforting as their own physical presence. He noted with some embarrassment that the sound of the pipes of Scotland had made Miss Fiona Elliott shed a tear; and he cleared his throat noisily to say, 'The fact they're near is a blessing, Miss Elliott.'

She turned and stared. 'Even if they're going away?'

That, he found, was disconcerting. Lamely he said, 'Oh, there'll be a reason. There always is.'

'Well, I wonder what it is this time. Do you happen to know, Mr Wilberforce?'

'Well, I – er – no, I don't really, Miss Elliott.' He tried desperately. 'Perhaps a misunderstanding...'

She turned her face away, towards her mother, Lady Mary. Her shoulders were heaving ... it was most embarrassing. And Mr Wilberforce had a growing feeling that he was being snubbed and that his presence was unwelcome. Women were very odd, very odd indeed.

In Calcutta, before finalising the orders to the Commander-in-Chief, the Viceroy had called a council. The illustrious members had been horrified at the indication that the train might be attacked and the lives of the hostages thus placed in fearful jeopardy. Lord Elgin was forced to moderate his instructions; and fresh orders, this time from Elgin in his official capacity as Governor-General in Council, reached Sir George

White. These orders were at once passed on by whatever means were available. The First Division was still upon the march westwards and Fettleworth was still on the lookout, through his scouts and picquets, for signs of his quarry now so well in rear of his advance, when a subaltern was seen riding in from the extended scouting party on the right flank. This subaltern was accompanied by another rider, a civilian apparently. The two men cantered up to Fettleworth; the subaltern saluted and the civilian identified himself.

'Pollinger, General, British Resident in Chapra.'

'Ha! What do you want of me, may I ask, Mr Pollinger?'

'I have a despatch,' Pollinger said. 'Received by the telegraph from Calcutta, sir, the line having been restored—'

'For me, from His Excellency?'

'From the Commander-in-Chief,' Pollinger said, and produced the transcription, handing it to Fettleworth.

Fettleworth read it, his colour deepening as he did so. He flourished the piece of paper at his Chief of Staff. 'I'm ordered back to Bundarbar,' he said. 'Those damn Pathans have taken the train – and are uttering damn threats, by God!'

'Are we to attack, sir?' Lakenham asked.

'No, more's the pity! We're simply to stand

by. The passengers, Lakenham—'
'Hostages?'
Bloody Francis gave a grim nod. 'Yes! A safe conduct out of India with the gold. Pass the word at once, if you please, Lakenham. The division's to right wheel and make back to the east once again, and every care is to be exercised upon our arrival at Bundarbar. No provocation of the blasted tribesmen.' Fettleworth turned to Pollinger, waiting politely on his horse like a telegram boy. 'Thank you, Mr Pollinger, I'm obliged. You may return to Chapra ... and kindly send a despatch to Sir George White in Calcutta. He may rely upon me. I shall do my utmost to safeguard the hostagcs.'

Pollinger rode back towards Chapra, and the First Division executed its turn to the shouts of the sergeant-majors and colour-sergeants, and of the company and squadron Sergeant-Majors from the engineers and the cavalry, the creak of leathcr, thc rattle of rifle-slings and sidc-arms and the neighing of the horses.

Blaise-Willoughby had been desperately anxious about Wolseley: true, the lcg had been splinted but he was no veterinary and he could have botched the job, and if so that might mean that poor Wolseley would have a permanent limp, might even be no longer able to sit comfortably upon his shoulder.

That would be a poor reward for a monkey that had, in effect, found the gold bullion and stood fair to save the Raj thereby. Blaise-Willoughby hurried down towards the plain, with Wolseley cradled in his arms like a baby. He scowled when he reflected that there were those at Division, Bloody Francis himself being one, who had no love for poor Wolseley, regarding him merely as a peanut-scattering pest. Bloody Francis was always particularly anti-Wolseley, almost pathologically so. Poor, harmless little animal ... Blaise-Willoughby hurried on, and hurried too much.

He tripped on a jag of rock in his haste, and he pitched headlong. There was intense pain as a leg curled beneath his body: and when he tried to get up, he couldn't. His leg was as broken as was Wolseley's. Blaise-Willoughby clenched his teeth and uttered a stream of blasphemies. It was a long way to Chapra; the gold would have to wait. And so would Wolseley. And he might not be found before he died: India was a cruel land. It was too bad.

Some while after Brora had recovered consciousness in his stinking dungeon, sounds came through, faintly enough but audible if he listened keenly. At first they were confused, and so was he, and he was unable to interpret what they might mean. He believed there were a number of men close at hand; he couldn't quite make out whether they were above him or beside him, but eventually he settled for a belief that they were above him. Both walls and ceiling must be extremely thick, Brora thought; he could hear no actual footfalls. The sound was probably reaching him via the door, which was also thick, but was naturally not made of solid stone.

After listening for some time Brora heard rifle shots, and within half a minute of hearing them he heard a voice, raised loud, a voice that he recognised unmistakably though he couldn't distinguish the words: *the voice was Ogilvie's.*

Help, then, was not far away – was very close! Brora struggled in his bonds, moved his lips and teeth with difficulty behind the gagging cloth that was keeping him silent. His thoughts now were red and angry: if Ogilvie had any damn sense or initiative he would have found this filthy dungeon and released his Major. But he hadn't and didn't. Time passed, and the sounds from above faded. More sound came back later, but this time it was a different sound: the door was being opened up. Someone unseen entered, and as the door creaked open Brora saw nothing but darkness beyond. As the door closed again tinder was struck and a tallow lamp was lit. A Pathan stood there, a *jezail* in his hands. The man stared down at Brora. In Pushtu he said, 'A use for you may come shortly, Major sahib. The Raj is so far being obstinate.'

That was all; Brora was unable to ask questions through the gag. The Pathan squatted on the floor, watchfully, the *jezail* laid across his knees, jaws moving rhythmically as he chewed betel nut. The tallow lamp remained alight. Now and again the Pathan spat a stream of purple juice towards Brora. The very air seemed filled with menace and Brora, wondering to what use he was to be put, began to sweat freely. He was going to need much courage. All this was a different kettle of fish from the field of battle and the whirling broadsword.

Fifteen

'I'm damned if I know yet what I shall do,' Bloody Francis said. 'I shall decide upon arrival at Bundarbar.'

'It's advisable to have a plan ready,' Lakenham said.

'Nonsense. One always changes one's plans in the end.'

'Then you need your alternatives ready, sir.'

Fettleworth shifted irritably in his saddle. 'Oh, damn, very well, then! What do *you* suggest, Lakenham?' He had the air of someone putting the ball very firmly back into an opponent's court.

'I think basically we must decide what to do if we're fired upon.'

'Fire back.'

'Not necessarily, sir. That is why I think some plan is wanted. What have we to consider?' Lakenham answered his own question as the Divisional Commander's mouth sagged open indecisively. 'We have to consider, first of all, the hostages—'

'No, we haven't. We have to consider the

Raj first of all.'

Lakenham, his point about a plan now well and truly scored, said, 'But surely, sir, the Raj and the hostages are intertwined, as it were?'

'What?'

'When you consider the one, you consider the other at the same time. In a sense the hostages *are* the Raj—'

'Oh, balls, Lakenham! The hostages, poor souls, and I'm far from blaming them, are acting against the Raj by the very fact of their being there at all in that damn train! If they weren't damn well there, all this would never have arisen, would it?'

'I don't see that such thoughts help at all,' Lakenham answered tartly. 'We must face the facts as they are.'

'Facts are a damn nuisance.'

'Indeed they are, very often. But they happen to exist, sir, and—'

'Well, go on,' Bloody Francis said belligerently. 'Suggest something, for heaven's sake!'

'I have already suggested, my dear sir, that you settle your mind and your division's on the question of what we do if we're fired upon.'

'We won't be. I'm far too powerful.'

'Let me hypothesise, sir,' Lakenham said loudly, bringing his riding-crop down with a slap on his knee-boots. Bloody Francis grew more and more impossible as day succeeded day. 'I suggest that we *may* be fired upon, not that we *will* be. If so, it is essential that we decide whether or not to retaliate. Do you not agree?'

'I have already made up my mind on that point, Lakenham, thank you. As I think I have in fact said, I shall answer shot with shot.'

'I see. Do you really think that's wise?'

'If I had not, I would not have said it.'

'Ah-ha,' Lakenham said non-committally. 'The despatch from Calcutta urged discretion, sir. To retaliate is not discretion and I would advise that we turn the other cheek—'

'You may turn what you wish, Lakenham, but I shall not.'

'In the best interest of the hostages, sir.'

'The hostages?'

'The hostages.'

'And what about the Raj, pray?'

Lakenham breathed hard down his nose. 'We have already been into that, General. I must really insist on the vital importance of the hostages' safety. Calcutta was very precise on the point, at any rate until matters clarify.' Lakenham paused. 'We must not forget the presence aboard the train of women and children, sir.'

'No, indeed. Or of old Farrar-Drumm. Be assured that I have no intention of forgetting them! But I shall not act as a namby-pamby cowardy custard, Lakenham. Turn the other cheek, pish! Damn it all, you're nothing but an old woman!'

Haughtily, General Fettleworth rode on. His Chief of Staff was a blasted nuisance, constantly nit-picking. And here he was, at it again: Fettleworth, Lakenham said, should bear in mind the advisability, on arrival at Bundarbar station, of initially holding the division at a circumspect distance from the enemy and sending a party forward under a flag of truce. The Pathans would be most unlikely to open upon a flag of truce since it was their own expressed wish to negotiate. General Fettleworth gave a sniff but no other answer. He was immensely angry; in point of fact he had already decided upon this course of action but now it was too late to say so and afterwards Lakenham would claim it as his own idea...

Trundling across the Indian plain, through the still sticky and clinging mud, the First Division went eventually into night bivouacs on the advice of the Divisional Medical Officer, and Lakenham did not argue this time: the soldiers, having been sent this way and that by the changes of orders, were badly in need of a respite; and so were the horses, and the mules and camels of the commissariat and ammunition columns.

After a night's rest an early start was made with the next dawn, and the First Division rumbled on. By mid-morning, the advanced scouts sent a rider back to report Bundarbar station in distant view; and at noon precisely the van of the division came to a prudent halt some half-mile south of the train. As it did so, a trewed officer was seen coming from the direction of the bridge across the Ganges; the bridge appeared, via Fettleworth's binoculars, to be held by a small body of Scots, much to the Divisional Commander's astonishment.

As the officer approached, Fettleworth recognised Ogilvie.

'Well, Captain Ogilvie! Bless my soul! I am much astounded. What are you doing here, my boy?'

Ogilvie explained as briefly as possible. Fettleworth demanded his full report, and he gave a comprehensive one of his prior movements, adding that Blaise-Willoughby had gone off on a gold hunt, an item that seemed to excite Fettleworth immensely notwithstanding the needle in a haystack element. Ogilvie indicated that the train was strongly held, but not to the extent of engaging a whole division. On the other hand, he said, it was his belief that any attempt to board would mean the deaths of the hostages. His report given, Fettleworth dismissed him back to the bridge without any precise orders, after which the flag-of-truce party, already detailed whilst on the march, prepared to ride forward. Lakenham himself was to ride with them at his own insistence; a high-ranking officer, he said, was needed and it would be unwise for the General to go himself.

'Well, of course!' Fettleworth snapped. 'Why have a dog and bark yourself?' Sitting his horse, he watched the party ride away, and saw a number of ragged tribesmen leave the vicinity of the train and ride to meet them. The conference, if such was the word, didn't last long: Lakenham was back at Fettleworth's side within little more than five minutes.

'Well?' Bloody Francis demanded.

'Not well at all, sir—'

'Why the hell not, Lakenham? Why the hell not?'

'Give me a chance, sir, if you please. The Pathans merely re-stated their position as indicated to Calcutta. They will make no concessions whatsoever. Either the gold bullion is guaranteed free passage into Afghanistan or the hostages will die. When the guarantee is given, men will be left behind to continue holding the hostages until word comes back that the gold is safely across the Frontier.'

'Hah! It'll be certain death for any Pathan left behind, I fancy!'

'Death before dishonour, sir, is a well-known Pathan precept. They have no fear of death.' Lakenham paused. 'As it is, matters have worsened for us.'

'Eh? How?'

'They've set a time limit. Calcutta must concede by 9 a.m. tomorrow.'

'Oh dear, oh dear!' Fettleworth blew out his cheeks. 'Has Calcutta been informed of this?'

Lakenham nodded. 'Yes. The Pathans have used the telegraph.'

'Ah, then we can await orders from Calcutta, of course! That makes things easier.' There was much relief in Fettleworth's voice. 'Fall out the men, Lakenham. They may smoke, and make tea. They may take luncheon ... I shall show the blasted tribesmen that I am prepared to act peacefully in the first instance.'

Lakenham gave his General a cynical look. The imperial bombast seemed to have evaporated.

The flag-of-truce proceedings and the First Division itself were a little beyond the range of Sir Clarence Farrar-Drumm's eyesight and by this time he was not on speaking terms with his ADC. He called down the coach.

'Sar'nt-Major!'

'Sir!'

'What is happening, Sar'nt-Major?'

'General Fettleworth's division, sir, is falling out by the look of it.'

'What!'

'Taking a meal, sir. The field kitchens are being set up, sir.'

'General Fettleworth's not marching in, Sar'nt-Major?' Farrar-Drumm's voice was disbelieving.

'No, sir, he is not.'

'Gad!'

Farrar-Drumm strained in his ropes. The modern army contained too many lilywhite livers for his liking. There was a weak spirit around. Naturally, Fettleworth would have to consider the safety of the hostages, but that shouldn't be allowed to dictate a yellow-belly approach. Fettleworth was all blow and no do; there he was, with his massive force that could have wiped out the Pathans as fast as dammit, and what did he do? He had lunch.

'Sar'nt-Major!'

'Sir!'

'Is there any sign of Southern Army?'

'Not so far as I can see, sir.'

Farrar-Drumm gloomed. If Southern Army marched in, by Gad, they would show Fettleworth a trick or two! He strained again at his bonds, his fighting spirit surging. He would escape somehow or other, and lead his men in while Fettleworth slept off his lunch. He thought once more, sadly, about the Welsh at Ulundi. Taffies, that was what they called them. Good men ... there had been very little to eat at Ulundi.

Lord Dornoch shaded his eyes against the glare of noon: a man was doubling back, one of the picquets posted distantly to the north of his line of advance as the Royal Strathspey, by now beginning to approach Dassar, continued with the relief work in the wake of the floods. The man came in, slammed to the halt, and saluted.

'Sir!'

'What is it, McGraw?'

'Smoke, sir. Smoke below the hills to the north, sir.'

'What sort of smoke?'

Private McGraw said, 'It's fading now, but it had the look of a signal, sir.'

'Had it, indeed! How far off?'

'It's in the plain at the foot of the hills, sir, and around eight miles off by Corporal Wood's estimate, sir.'

Lord Dornoch nodded; he was already looking through his field glasses but could see nothing. He said, 'Very well, back to the picquet, McGraw, and tell Corporal Wood I shall investigate.' He turned to the Adjutant. 'Captain Black, detach a corporal and four men. They can take wagon horses, and I'll halt the column for a stand easy.'

Black saluted smartly and turned his horse down the line of advance, calling orders. The Scots fell out for a smoke and to ease weary, sweaty feet, lying or sitting on the muddy ground to the detriment of their kilts. They were all fed up to the eyeballs with disinfectation and they were all scared by the possibility of disease spreading. They preferred action; there was hope that the strange smoke-signal, word of which had now reached all ranks, might in some way have them drawn off what they were now calling the lice patrol. So there was eagerness for the return of the mounted party; and there was excitement when, within a couple of hours or so, the men were seen riding back. As they came closer, a body could be seen laid across the saddle of the corporal in charge, while another man carried what looked like a small monkey with which he was having considerable difficulty; his face was badly scratched. The party rode up to the Colonel, and the corporal reported.

'A sick man, sir, apparently British. We found him unconscious, sir, some distance east of where a fire of brushwood had been lit – around half a mile from the foothills and making apparently in the direction of Chapra, sir, according to his tracks.'

'Any other signs of life, Corporal?'

'None, sir, neither in the hills nor in the

plain. And no other fresh tracks, sir, though there appeared to have been riders heading south some while earlier.' The corporal paused. 'I believe the man fell and hit his head after lighting the fire, sir. There was blood on a nasty jagged rock, sir, where his head lay.'

Dornoch nodded. 'Thank you, Corporal. That's a full report.'

'Thank you, sir. There is also a monkey, sir.'

'So I observed!' Memory was stirring in Dornoch's mind: he knew of only one man in Northern India who was invariably accompanied by a monkey. He walked across to the corporal's horse and looked at the man who was being lifted down by the medical orderlies under Surgeon Major Corton.

'Blaise-Willoughby!' he said. 'What's the matter with him, Doctor?'

'He has a broken leg, Colonel, and two bad gashes on his head, the second of very recent origin, I believe. And he's unconscious, as you can see,' Corton added.

'Serious?'

Corton shrugged. 'I can't say yet, Colonel.'

'Examine him as fast as you can, then, and let me have a report.' Dornoch went across to the man who held the monkey. He remembered its name now: Wolseley.

Wolseley, too, seemed to have a broken leg. Dornoch looked up at the private, who was still mounted. 'Where did you find him?' he asked.

'Sitting on the gentleman, sir.'

Dornoch laughed. 'Faithful!'

'Aye, sir. He wouldn't be moved, not at first, sir. He's vicious, sir, and you'd best have a care.'

'I think you're right! Report to the medical section, right away. Those bites could be dangerous.'

'Aye, sir.'

Dornoch turned away. Shortly after this the Surgeon Major came up with the Adjutant and gave his report. Blaise-Willoughby, he confirmed, was badly concussed, no doubt as a result of a fall whilst trying to walk with a broken leg.

'But why the fire, the apparent smoke signal?' Dornoch asked in some perplexity. 'You'd think, having lit it, he'd stay by it!'

Black answered before the Doctor. 'Impatience, perhaps, Colonel. A feeling that it was not going to be seen. And he may have been trying to make towards us, if he'd seen us.'

'Yes, perhaps.' Dornoch turned again to the Surgeon Major. 'You used the word walk, Doctor. *Can* a man walk with a broken leg?'

'Hop rather than walk, I would imagine,

Colonel! And that's a thought in itself.'
'Why?'
Corton said, 'I would expect a man with a broken leg to crawl – to drag himself along. Doing that, he'd not fall. But to hop ... along with what the Adjutant has just said, I deduce a need for speed. There was urgency, Colonel.'
'Yes, that seems obvious enough!' Dornoch frowned. 'How long before he's able to tell us what the urgency was?'
Corton shrugged. 'That's impossible to say, Colonel. It could be soon, but I believe not. I've known men lie for as long as two weeks in deep unconsciousness.'
'And then?'
'Then they've died. I've known cases where it's been possible to penetrate the unconsciousness by shouting very loudly.'
'Did that bring out an answer, Doctor?'
'Sometimes. Not always.'
'Worth a try,' Dornoch said crisply. 'Start your shouting, Doctor, if you please, and if your voice is not loud enough, bring up a colour-sar'nt! You know who Blaise-Willoughby is, I take it?'
'I know the man well, Colonel.'
'Then you'll understand my need. Political Officers have a tendency to impinge very sharply on current events, and I have a feeling that there may be something important inside Blaise-Willoughby's head that must

be brought out.' Dornoch turned to Captain Black. 'The battalion will remain at rest until further orders,' he said. 'If Major Blaise-Willoughby's mind can't be penetrated, we'll march on for Dassar, which is possibly where those other tracks led.'

During the afternoon, Bloody Francis had come to certain conclusions and had changed his mind as a result. To wait for word from Calcutta might be considered procrastination. The telegraph was not always a swift instrument; it was subject to many faults and breaks, to many delays and often enough to incomprehensibility as well. Also, Viceroys took time to reach decisions, sometimes deliberately so that someone else was landed with the responsibility. That someone was invariably the senior officer on the spot, in this case he, Fettleworth, himself. If in the meantime he was judged to be content to sit back and wait, much blame would be thrust in at his door if matters went astray. Therefore, he would do a little probing.

'What sort of probing, sir?' Lakenham asked.

'A thrust at the damn Pathans, that's what! Just to find out the reaction. They could be bluffing.'

'I am quite sure they are not bluffing, sir. They have everything at stake.'

'Yes, so have the hostages as I've said before,' Bloody Francis stated in a bald lie: there was, Lakenham thought, no coping with his General's contradictory changes of direction or his chameleon-like ability to convince himself that none of them was a volte-face. 'I have to do my best for them. That's my duty, is it not?'

'Of course—'

'Well, then! Kindly don't always argue with me, Lakenham, I don't like it. I shall ride myself towards the train and see what that produces.'

'I would have a care, sir, if I were you.'

'I shall feel perfectly safe. They're most unlikely to open fire upon me. We are present in far too much strength for them if we should mount an attack, and I believe that even the hostages would not prevent the men surging forward if they should see their General fall.'

Lakenham opened his mouth, then shut it again; Bloody Francis was much too convinced of his popularity with the rank and file to be persuaded of the opposite. Had his words held any truth at all, Lakenham would have felt obliged to point out that to invite a Pathan bullet would scarcely be in the best interests of the hostages. But since he feared no surge from the troops he held his peace; the fact that Fettleworth was unlikely to achieve anything by his ride was immaterial. It could probably do no harm; and up to a point Lakenham understood. To do anything was better than doing nothing, and indeed there was a restive atmosphere throughout the whole division by this time.

Fettleworth said, 'There is no time like the present, Lakenham, and I shall advance immediately. I shall take you and my ADC, and no one else. When I am within a dozen yards of the train, you will both fall back and leave me.'

'You'll take a flag of truce, sir?'

'No.'

'If you don't—'

'I am not offering a parley, Lakenham, I am a probe.'

There was no more to be said; probe and escort left the encampment of the First Division and rode forward, rode as it were into the unknown. As they were seen to approach, the Pathans' perimeter guards lifted their *jezails* and closed in towards the party to block its way. The Pathan leader appeared in one of the train doors. Fettleworth called out, 'I come peacefully. As you see, I do not bring in my soldiers. Only myself.'

'And your purpose, General sahib?'

Fettleworth frowned, hummed and ha'ed for a moment, then spoke aside to Lakenham. 'Damn! What's my purpose, Lakenham?'

Lakenham snapped, 'God knows, sir, I do not!'

'I don't call that helpful.'

'I'm sorry, sir. I suggest you say that you wish to satisfy yourself that the hostages are being properly treated.'

'So that I can reassure Calcutta ... yes, Lakenham, you've hit it on the head! A very good idea. I can ride down the coaches, and look through the windows. You may fall back now.' Fettleworth urged his horse forward, clear of the Chief of Staff and the ADC. He called out, 'I ask permission to inspect the hostages, so that I may assure Calcutta that they are well.'

'You are welcome to do so, General sahib,' the Pathan leader called back, grinning. Fettleworth rode ahead, slowly and ponderously, then turned his horse along the track to ride first down the front coaches. He looked in through the windows as he passed along, sucking in his cheeks as he saw the bound hostages, the pale, wan faces of the women and children. He met the staring eyes of Sir Clarence Farrar-Drumm; Farrar-Drumm was obviously wishing to communicate but was prevented by one of the Pathans who laid a knife at his throat. Fettleworth rode on; the coaches were filled with the tribesmen from Afghanistan, virtually one Pathan to each of the passengers, ready and waiting with their knives. In an attack, the hostages wouldn't have a hope. Each would die in the very moment that the First Division moved in. And Fettleworth read in the faces and the staring eyes that the hostages knew this only too well.

In silence he rode back to join his Chief of Staff. He felt the experience had been useful enough.

'They're suffering, Lakenham,' he said gruffly, 'and there's nothing to be done about it. At least I've satisfied myself that I can't possibly attack. One can only hope the Pathans'll not risk the vengeance of the Raj when it comes to the point.'

'You mean—'

'I mean the point of refusal to concede, Lakenham! Sir George is right – we cannot concede. And we cannot attack! It's a cleft stick. The only hope for the hostages is that in the last resort the Pathans are bluffing. They must know that if they kill the hostages, they'll be slaughtered to a man within minutes.'

Sixteen

The night, the night before the final decision had to be made, wore away in mounting tension. At a little before midnight, a mounted runner had come in from Patna with word received via the telegraph from Calcutta: Bloody Francis was to use every endeavour to have the 9 a.m. limit extended so that further advices might be sought from Whitehall. Procrastination was the order of the day now; the affair had to be dragged out in the hope that the Pathans would lose heart when their demands were not quickly conceded and when they began to reflect upon the immense power of the Raj as represented by Fettleworth's division camped on their very doorstep.

Once again, Fettleworth rode out, this time with a flag of truce waving in the light from the guard lanterns, and with a General's escort of the cavalry. He demanded a parley, and he got it. The Pathan leader rode forward to meet him, also accompanied by an escort.

'What does the General sahib wish?' the

leader asked.

'A delay.'

'There will be no delay. By nine o'clock, the decision must be made.'

Fettleworth said, 'In your own interests, I advise delay.'

There was a pause; then the Pathan asked, 'Why is this, General sahib?'

'The Raj cannot lightly allow gold bullion to be stolen. There must be consultation with the government of Her Majesty the Queen-Empress in Whitehall. This takes time. If you do not allow time enough, then the decision must be taken by His Excellency the Viceroy alone. It will be his duty to refuse your demands.'

'And this, His Excellency has said?'

'Yes,' Fettleworth answered boldly, and quaked in his saddle. His Excellency had said no such thing, and might well resent the statement later on. However, the lie appeared to have its hoped-for effect. There was another pause, while the Pathan consulted with his henchmen; there was much muttering, and heads were shaken and nodded. What the General sahib had said held the ring of sense. All consultations took time, and to compromise often led to success.

'How much delay is asked?' the Pathan called.

'As long as it may take. I ask that the time

limit be scrapped, and that you await a response from Calcutta, which will be given to you by myself as soon as consultations are complete.'

A laugh floated back through the lantern-lit darkness. The General sahib was asking the ridiculous, the Pathan said. 'We would be kept waiting until the Prophet came again, until all men's beards were long enough to stretch from here to Kabul. The time limit will be delayed for one more dawn, and that is all.'

The Pathans turned about and rode away. 'That's not long enough!' Fettleworth called after them agitatedly. There was no response. With nothing more to be done, Fettleworth and his escort rode back into the encampment and the mounted runner was despatched back to Patna with his tidings for the telegraph.

During the night more men came to Lord Brora in his damp dungeon, entering as circumspectly as the man with the guarding *jezail*, still squatting on the floor, had done earlier. A lantern was shone directly into Brora's eyes and one of the men unfastened the gag from his mouth and said, 'Now you will help us, Major sahib.'

'Will I!' Brora made strange faces, stretching his lips.

'We believe you will, yes.'

'Really. In what way?'

The man said, 'When first we captured you, it was luck ... the luck sent by Allah and his intermediary the Prophet. Since then you have told us who you are. And we have learned other things also.'

'What things?' Brora glared into the light.

'That you have your womenfolk aboard the train, Major sahib.'

Brora gave a start; he whitened, then swore. 'What is that to you?' he asked.

He was answered with a laugh. 'Much! And it is much to *you*, I believe—'

'Are you singling them out for some special unpleasantness?' Brora asked. 'Is that what you're saying?'

'Not if there is co-operation, Major sahib. If there is not...' The Pathan had no need to put it into words. 'You, Major sahib, are by your own statement a peer of the British realm, and as such you undoubtedly carry much authority and command much respect. As an officer of the Raj, your word is trusted. You tell the truth, and in the telling of it you do not give undue weight to your personal position—'

'You mean my niece and sister-in-law?'

'Yes, I mean this.'

Brora licked at his lips. 'What are you asking of me?'

There was a pause, then the Pathan said, 'Your government in Calcutta has asked for a delay in our time limit, which was to be nine o'clock tomorrow. This we have given, a delay of one day only. I swear to you upon the souls of my ancestors, and upon the Prophet Mohammed, and upon Allah, that this delay is all we shall give and that it will not be extended again. By the time the hands of the clock reach nine hours on the morning after the next one, the people in the train will die by the *jezail* and the bayonet if our demands have not been met. If I do not speak the truth, then may my soul live in torment for a thousand years.' There was another pause. 'Do you believe me, Major sahib?'

With reluctance, Brora nodded. Truth and a fanatical determination were clear in the Pathan's eyes; there was no room for doubt. Brora said, 'Yes. I believe you.'

'I am glad. I think the Raj does not as yet. I think the Raj hopes that we are bluffing. I believe the Raj will take risks on this hope, and that they will attack us when they are ready to do so. This is perhaps what they are asking the Queen-Empress to decide for them. This attack may come even before the end of the time set.'

Brora's eyes gleamed. 'And I?'

'You, Major sahib, will speak to the General sahib commanding the soldiers by the train, and tell him that bluff is not in our minds. You must make him understand that attack means death for the hostages before our own deaths. Of this, he must be made very clear. This you will do.'

'Will I indeed?'

The Pathan said, 'I do not wish to return to the matter of your womenfolk, Major sahib. You will do as I have said. If it is necessary, you will prepare a message for the telegraph to Calcutta.'

'I'll need to be released, won't I?' Brora said.

The Pathan nodded. 'This is so. It matters not. Your usefulness lies with the British now, not with us. And you can do no harm to us, as is obvious. In a few minutes from now, you will be free to go. But remember this: from this moment on, a special watch will be kept on your women aboard the train.'

Ogilvie, meanwhile, was walking with Colour-Sergeant MacTrease, picking his way through the lines of sleeping bodies on the bridge spanning the moonlit Ganges. It was a long bridge, for here the river was wide. The water, though no longer as high as it had been, and contained now within its banks, was still moving fast and bringing down all manner of debris, pieces of wood, clothing, the inevitable bodies, bloated and grotesque. Ogilvie stopped when not far from the south bank and looked out towards the train, no more than half a mile away and fully visible for most of its length. On its far side Fettleworth's camp fires burned redly; there was any amount of strength handy to finish off the Pathans. Ogilvie's breath hissed through his teeth: the whole business was one of sheer frustration. He had been sent word by Fettleworth as to the Pathans' time limit; it was still not known what Calcutta would do when that time limit expired. Just how valuable was the gold and the prestige of the Raj? Ogilvie was about to ask the question for the hundredth time, rhetorically, of MacTrease when the Colour-Sergeant said in a whisper, 'Captain Ogilvie, sir, look down there, by the river bank.'

'What is it, Colour?'

'Men, sir, down by the end abutment, the support pier. Do you see them, sir?'

Ogilvie looked down; the moon was bright and he saw shadowy figures making their way apparently from below the bridge itself towards the south-east. One of them appeared to be a British officer: the moon shone in pin-pricks of light from badges and buckles; and then Ogilvie saw the trewed legs, clear in the moonlight.

'One of ours!' he said in amazement.

'Aye, sir, and by the huge size of him, it's the Major – and being taken, I'd say, sir, though God knows where he appeared from in the first place—'

Ogilvie was already running ahead with his revolver drawn. Close behind him, MacTrease followed with his rifle held across his chest. They remained unseen for a brief while only; as they reached the end of the bridge a *jezail* fired, and a bullet snicked the stonework of the parapet. MacTrease fired back and scored a bull's-eye: a Pathan fell, and rolled down into the Ganges. The others disappeared, shadows merging with the night. Brora stood there, silhouetted by the moonlight against the water, tall and powerful.

'What's going on, Major?' Ogilvie called.

'So it's you, is it, Ogilvie? I thought I heard your voice earlier.'

'Where have you been?'

'Held prisoner in what I now see to be the bridge abutment,' Brora called. 'Stay where you are, Ogilvie. I'm coming up to join you.'

Brora strode powerfully through the night, climbed to the roadway running onto the bridge, and came forward like a tiger, his eyes gleaming in the silver light of the moon. He was plainly an angry man. Striding towards Ogilvie and MacTrease he said, 'My niece and her mother are aboard that train. But of course you're aware of that.'

'Yes, Major.'

'Those black buggers are putting them under special threat, unless I do what they ask of me.' Briefly, Brora explained, and added, 'I see no military reason why I shouldn't go to Fettleworth and pass on the Pathans' message – since it happens to be true that they're not bluffing. Or so I'm convinced. Fettleworth might just as well know. Do you agree?'

'Why do you ask, Major? I'm not—'

'I ask, because I shall be doing something that might be misconstrued later. I shall be doing what I have been told to do by the enemy – do you understand me? I could be accused of putting my womenfolk before my duty.'

Ogilvie said, 'I wouldn't see it in that light, Major. I would consider it your duty to put all relevant knowledge before General Fettleworth. All decisions afterwards are up to him.'

Brora nodded. 'Yes. Thank you for that, Ogilvie. It helps to outweigh the damn harm you may have done to my niece and my sister-in-law—'

'Harm? How, Major?'

Brora said harshly, 'By opening fire on those natives. It'll have been noted aboard the train.' He gave Ogilvie no chance to respond; he turned on his heel and walked off the bridge, fast, making towards Division on the far side of the railway station. Ogilvie stared after him, feeling a cold stab of fear in his belly. Brora was right: trouble might come now for Fiona, and if it did, it would have come through his own act. But his duty had been plain: Brora had appeared to be in Pathan hands and there could have been only the one reaction to that. The thought, however, failed to help. Ogilvie clenched his hands; the finger-nails dug hard into his palms. Until MacTrease spoke to him, urgently, he was unaware of his surroundings and of a sudden dramatic change in the temperature.

MacTrease asked in a puzzled voice, 'Do you feel it, sir?' He had to repeat the question twice.

Ogilvie turned away from his sight of the train. 'Feel what, Colour?' Then he noticed it for himself: a wind had come up, blowing from the west, and it was a curiously warm wind, most unusual for a night wind, and it seemed to be blowing steadily, very steadily. 'What do you make of it, Colour?' he asked.

MacTrease said, 'I don't know, sir. I've not known anything quite the same ... it's like a wind coming off a fire, sir, and bringing the heat with it.'

'Chapra on fire?'

'I don't know, sir, but that's what it feels like to me, sir.'

Fettleworth had been aroused from his sleep to hear Lord Brora's report; he received it grumpily and with foreboding: he had been banking on bluff, and he had a suspicion that His Excellency had as well. 'Are you positive, Major?' he asked, pulling his uniform tunic over his pyjamas.

'Absolutely so, General. I have no doubt in my mind at all.'

'Damn!'

'The Pathans know they're all for the rope now whatever happens – they've nothing more to lose.'

'But everything to gain if we concede.' Bloody Francis put his head in his hands and groaned. 'What a diabolic situation! Quite diabolic.'

'Yes, indeed. May I ask what you propose to do about it, General?'

'I don't know. I must consider. Frankly, at this moment I envisage no change in my plans, Major.'

'I see.' There was a sneer in Brora's voice. 'May I ask, sir, what *were* your plans?'

'To wait and see.' Bloody Francis threw up his hands in a gesture of utter despair. 'What else can one do?' He was about to utter further words of indecision when something curious happened: his tent seemed to lean sideways, or was it the ground? He didn't know; he looked up at his Chief of Staff, who was standing just inside the flap and was also leaning, or so it appeared.

'What is happening, Lakenham? Is it—'

'An earth tremor, sir. Quite distinct.'

Fettleworth gasped. 'You're sure?'

'I am in no doubt at all, sir. I've experienced such things before. I suggest you rouse out the men without delay, by the bugle.'

'But the blasted Pathans, Lakenham – they'll assume I'm about to attack—'

'I doubt it, sir, since they will have felt the movement also.' Not waiting for Fettleworth to make up his mind, the Chief of Staff went out through the tent flap and a moment later the bugles were sounding loud and clear over the bivouacs.

Seventeen

General Farrar-Drumm, down whose side-whiskers a trail of saliva was running, awoke with a start. 'Gad! The bugles! Fettleworth's come to his senses at last. He's attacking, Smyth!'

Captain Smyth, pleased to be spoken to once again, was yet obliged to disagree. 'I think it's the earthquake, sir. General Fettleworth is—'

'Earthquake? What earthquake, Smyth? There's been no blasted earthquake!'

'A tremor, sir—' Captain Smyth broke off as the train gave a very distinct heave. He clutched at the side of his seat. 'There, sir.'

'Yes, see what yer mean. I don't like this, damned if I do. The whole damn train could fall into the earth and us with it.' Farrar-Drumm raised his voice to call along the crowded coach. 'Sar'nt-Major!'

'Sir?'

'There's an earthquake in progress, Sar'nt-Major.'

'Aye, sir,' Cunningham called back. He wondered what the General expected him to do about it, but no further shouts came. Cunningham went on with what he had been doing, surreptitiously, for some while now: very gradually loosening the ropes that bound his wrists and held his body tight against the seat-back. Already there was a good deal of play. Hope had come to Cunningham: he was seeing the earth tremor as sent by God to the assistance of the hostages: the Pathans were rattled, and badly. Maybe, Cunningham thought, they were seeing wrath on the part of Mohammed, who had turned against them. Whatever it was, they were jabbering together and rolling their eyes and were clustering by the exit doors, all ready to leave in a hurry. One or two from other coaches, he saw from his window, had already jumped down to the track and were staring towards the west, whence was coming an extraordinarily warm wind. Cunningham could estimate their thoughts: the British bullets, should they come, would be one thing; to be swallowed into the bowels of the earth was quite another, and perhaps better faced in the open, where they could run from the gaping land, rather than closeted aboard a railway train. And they might just as well be outside in any case: already Cunningham had been told that the Pathans had explosives, and with his own eyes, from the windows he had observed certain preparations being put in hand. There had been much activity beneath the centre of the train and talk overheard had indicated a deal of coming and going between there and the signal box; Cunningham had a shrewd suspicion that the Pathans had no need to be physically present aboard the train when the moment came, if it did, to despatch the hostages. And this was something that should be reported to Division.

Cunningham strained away, the sweat pouring into his eyes. That wind was hot, very hot. Curious ... it might be connected with the earth tremors and again it might not, but Cunningham fancied it was and that that might well portend a full-scale earthquake.

'Calcutta should have been in touch by now,' Bloody Francis said. He was feeling tired; he was too old for night arousals and a subsequent period of hanging about waiting for an earthquake. There had been further tremors, some of them very alarming to be sure, and a deep chasm had appeared in the very centre of his bivouac area, fortunately without any injury to his men. 'They really should have sent precise instructions by now. White and His Excellency seem to be leaving the whole blasted thing to me!'

'It would appear so, sir,' Lakenham said.

Fettleworth, seated on a camp chair outside his tent, fidgeted irritably as he watched the dawn come up, very red and angry – and still that wretched hot wind to alarm him and make everything worse. He brooded in self-pity: there would have to go and be a blasted earthquake to add to everything else and make his task more difficult! If that earthquake should come in earnest, he could see no way in which to avoid it. He could march his division away, but he might march it into the centre of devastation. It had to be another case of wait and see; Fettleworth, on the principle of lightning not striking twice in the same place, felt that the safest spot would be that chasm, so he stuck to it like a leech. Time went on; Fettleworth, still worrying about Calcutta, began to grow hungry and called for the time of breakfast to be advanced.

'There might not be time later,' he grumbled. When the field kitchens had produced breakfast he fell to with a surprisingly hearty appetite considering his anxieties, and made short work of his kedgeree and his liver-and-bacon, beautifully done, just as he liked it. Much hot coffee drove it all down, and, drinking his third cup, Fettleworth had an idea.

'By God, Lakenham,' he said, 'why didn't I think of it earlier, I wonder!'

'Think of what, sir?'

'Why, the telegraph in the station – here in Bundarbar! We know it's working again. The Pathans used it to transmit their wretched demands to Calcutta, via Patna! Isn't that so?'

'Yes, sir, but—'

'No buts, Lakenham,' Bloody Francis said energetically. 'I'm going to ask the Pathans to allow me use of the telegraph in order to hurry Calcutta into a decision. They can't possibly refuse – it's in their own interest, after all! What do you think of that?'

'It could be tried, sir—'

'Of course it could, and will be.'

'But I fail to see very much point, frankly.'

'Point! Damn it, man, I'll be in touch with Calcutta, won't I?'

'His Excellency will send a message when he's ready, sir. Not before.'

'But he may have made up his mind by now, and I can get the message quicker than waiting for a damn runner from Patna, don't you see? If I don't get it soon, these blasted earth tremors may swallow up the runner. Besides, there's another thing: infiltration!'

'A Trojan horse?'

'Yes! Naturally, I won't go myself, but you can on my behalf, with an escort—'

'Which is unlikely to be allowed to carry arms, sir,' Lakenham pointed out. 'I can't see that any useful purpose will be served at all by a Trojan horse totally inhibited by a lack of weapons, but—'

'Damn you—'

'But if that's your order, sir, it will of course be carried out.'

Weary from his long exertions, Cunningham sat in the train with his hands all but free. Now, he was biding his time, which he felt would come soon. Most of the Pathans were now down upon the track; more had jumped down each time a tremor had come. The railway line had become a trifle bent and the coaches were leaning sideways, and that had really rattled the tribesmen. Not that there was any lack of vigilance; the natives surrounded the train, and the *jezails* and knives were ready yet. The gold still beckoned, there was no doubt about that at all. But with the Pathans out of the train, there was at least elbow room. The atmosphere was very tense nevertheless, and there was more fear in the faces of the women as the evidence of earthquake mounted. Some were crying, some sat with white, still faces as though resigned to the end, some were doing their best to keep up the spirits of the children.

Looking out of the window, Cunningham saw a mounted party approaching from Fettleworth's encampment: a red-tabbed general officer, with an escort and a signaller. A number of Pathans went out to meet this party, with their *jezails* aimed. The red-tabbed officer called out loudly enough for Cunningham to hear: 'I am Brigadier-General Lakenham, Chief of Staff to General Fettleworth. I ask your permission to use the telegraph, to send a message to Calcutta, and await an answer.'

One of the Pathans called back, 'What message is this?'

'To ask if His Excellency will agree to your demands.'

The Pathans conferred together; after a while the shout went back, 'You may come, but unarmed. Cast down your weapons.'

The party did so, and then rode forward into the mouths of the *jezails*. Cunningham sweated, wondering if the moment had come. He looked along the coach: no Pathans still, but plenty on the track. There was a new restiveness among the hostages now; they would be desperately anxious to know the result of the message to Calcutta. General Farrar-Drumm's head lolled; he was fast asleep, until Captain Smyth woke him up and told him what was happening. Then he, too, grew restive and agitated and kept peering from his window, and started an argument with his ADC. Two of the Pathans re-boarded the train and stood watching the hostages and fingering long, rusty knives, as though fearing some sort of upsurge while the British party was present in the station, however impossible an upsurge might be for bound men.

Cunningham settled back in his seat; the time hadn't yet come after all.

It was a long wait in the stationmaster's office. The Chief of Staff paced up and down, hands behind his back, glancing at the photographs of the late stationmaster's family. The morning wore away slowly, and the time for luncheon passed. Lakenham, too anxious to sit down passively, paced on. His escort waited outside. More tremors came, shaking the office. A photograph frame fell to the floor. A pane of glass shattered as though from a bullet, and the splinters fell in a shower. From the distance there came a low rumble; and the hot wind blew still, as if off the very fires of hell. His Excellency was taking his time; probably another council had been called, or word was still awaited from the India Office in distant Whitehall...

Brigadier-General Lakenham paced on into the afternoon. Fettleworth would be getting restive by this time; the ADC would be going through a rough patch with his lord and master. When Bloody Francis was truly anxious, he became more than impossible. When at last the reply from Calcutta began to come through, and was taken by the signaller from Division, it was accompanied by another earth tremor, a much larger one than any that had gone before. The office lurched sideways, then seemed to lift into the air and fall back again. The Pathan guards ran out into the open, their faces showing fear. Lakenham, clutching for support at the open door, saw that the telegraph was still, by some miracle, in operation. The signaller finished taking the message and turned to Lakenham.

'Message received, sir.'

'Well?'

'It reads, sir, there will be no concessions and you are free to mount an attack on the train at a moment of your own choosing prior to nine ack emma tomorrow. Every effort is to be made to safeguard the lives of the hostages.'

Lakenham met the signaller's eye: the die was now cast. He asked, 'And the originator?'

'His Excellency, sir, as Governor-General in Council.'

Lakenham nodded. 'We'll return to Division now. No questions from the Pathans are to be answered other than that the message was garbled and unreadable. Give it to me.'

The strip from the telegraph was handed over; Lakenham struck a match, put the flame to the paper, and watched it curl and blacken. No notice was being taken by the Pathans, who were too occupied with their fear of the coming earthquake. That earthquake, Lakenham thought, might yet offer the way out if the Pathans should run for safety, but if it came then no one, either British or Pathan, might live to see the next dawn. Outside the stationmaster's office Lakenham collected his escort and mounted his horse, which was rolling its eyes in fear of the unknown. The animal's nostrils were lifting dangerously, but Lakenham quietened it with soothing words, and rode for the perimeter. As he came down the side of the train, a face looked from a window and called out to him.

'General Lakenham, sir!'

The speaker was a warrant officer from a Scots battalion, the 114th. Lakenham said, 'Well, Sar'nt-Major, what is it?'

'Sir! My name is Cunningham, of—'

'I know your badges, Mr Cunningham. If you've something to say, say it fast.'

'Aye, sir. The train's to be blown up if an attack is mounted, sir—'

'How?'

'Dynamite, sir, a very large quantity beneath the central coach, and I believe there may be a fuse leading to the signal box at the western end of the station, sir.'

'I'll inform General Fettleworth at once, Sar'nt-Major,' Lakenham said, and added,

'I see you're free of your ropes. You'd better come back with me while the Pathans' attention is diverted, and make your own report.'

'No, sir, I'll not leave the women and children. That would not be right.'

Lakenham shrugged, his eyes watchful for any Pathan interest in the conversation: there appeared to be none. He said, 'It's up to you. I give no order either way.'

'I'll remain, sir. There are things I can do.'

'You're a brave man, Mr Cunningham.'

'It's no more than my duty, sir.' Cunningham hesitated. 'If I may ask this, sir: what is the answer from Calcutta?'

Lakenham looked him in the eyes, straight. 'You will keep this under your helmet, Sar'nt-Major. His Excellency has ordered the First Division to mount an attack. I can't say when this will come, but it will be before the time limit expires.' He touched his spurs lightly to the flanks of his horse, and rode towards the perimeter, where he was stopped by the Pathan leader in person.

'General sahib, you have spoken to Calcutta?'

'No. I was unable to read the reply,' Lakenham said. 'The earth tremors have upset the telegraph. May I now return to my division?'

He was allowed to go in peace; he had the

feeling, very strongly, that the Pathan had no doubts in his mind that Calcutta would concede in the final hour. As the Chief of Staff rode out from the Pathan line, the darkening day was lit by jagged streaks of lightning in the north.

'I'm relieved to have a decision, Lakenham, much relieved, but I don't like the task I've been set, damned if I do! I can't see how we can possibly safeguard the hostages – the less so in view of what Cunningham has reported.' Bloody Francis paused. 'I don't know, though! Could we not open with light artillery on the blasted signal box, and destroy it?'

'No, sir—'

'Why not, pray?'

Lakenham said, 'Because it would almost certainly light the fuse trail, if such exists.'

'Damn, yes.' Fettleworth pulled at his moustache. 'What about the Pathans? Do you suppose they'll bugger off if the earth tremors go on?'

'I'm unable to read their minds with any accuracy, sir, but at this moment they're there still and appear to be in full control of the train, though from outside rather than inside. What orders do you wish issued for the attack, sir, and when is it to be mounted?'

Fettleworth answered crossly. 'I dislike

being rushed, Lakenham. It's a momentous decision, quite momentous. Women and children...' His voice tailed off as a drumming sound started up from the canvas of his tent. 'What the devil's that, Lakenham?'

'Rain, sir.'

'Oh, God damn and blast, not more floods!'

'I'd sooner floods than earthquake,' Lakenham said grimly.

'Well, yes. Now – the question of attack. I propose, I think, not to use a sledgehammer – you know the saying, I cxpect—'

'Yes, sir.'

'A smaller force to start with, backed if necessary by my division. Do you agree?'

Lakenham frowned. 'Not fully, sir. A very heavy attack might be a better safeguard for the hostages, since it could roll over the Pathans before they could react. A small force wouldn't have the same effect, and might serve only to send the Pathans into action—'

'The explosives, d'you mean?'

'Yes. I would advise a large-scale assault, spearheaded by the cavalry—'

'Cavalry's no blasted use, Lakenham. They get their horses shot away, then their damn boots slow them up on foot so they make sitting targets.'

'I think you exaggerate, sir.'

'No, I don't.' Fettleworth looked around

the tent, then snapped his fingers and shouted for his bearer. When the man entered, salaaming, Fettleworth ordered *chota pegs* to be brought, and quickly. Then he turned again to his Chief of Staff. 'I'll send my infantry in with the bayonet to execute a frontal attack. I've no objection to using cavalry on the flanks to hem the buggers in when they start to run, and to round up any that get through the line. No more than that. And it might be a good thing to deploy a battalion round to the other side of the train, and thus mount an attack from both sides. How's that?'

Lakenham shook his head and sighed. Bloody Francis was a poor tactician. He said, 'No, sir. The deployed battalion would certainly be seen whilst attempting to outflank the train, and the element of surprise would be wholly lost.'

'Damn!' Fettleworth glowered for a moment, then brightened. 'Those Scots holding the bridge – the 114th. I can use them – they're positioned just right, by jove—'

'Company strength only, sir. Scarcely enough.'

Fettleworth breathed out angrily through his nostrils. 'You always cast down everything I say, Lakenham. You'd better make your own suggestions if you don't like mine!'

'Very well, sir. I suggest using Ogilvie's company of Scots, not to join the attack on the main body of Pathans, but simply to take the signal box. If they do that, then the explosive devices are put out of action immediately, and as soon as Ogilvie is in position, then the main attack goes in.'

'Yes, quite. I was about to suggest that myself, as a matter of fact,' Fettleworth said distantly. 'Kindly make the arrangements, Lakenham. We shall need time in which to prepare ... let me know as soon as you're ready.' The Divisional Commander turned his attention to *chota pegs*.

As soon as it was dark, a runner was despatched with orders for Ogilvie's company. In the meantime, aboard the train, the Regimental Sergeant-Major was making his own plans. Taking full advantage of the Pathans' preoccupation with the trembling earth, which in fact was currently somewhat more stable but might not remain so, Cunningham used his freedom from his ropes to move circumspectly along the coach and untie a number of his fellow-hostages, firstly the women and children, warning them to lie strictly doggo thereafter, and then Major-General Farrar-Drumm and Captain Smyth. Farrar-Drumm was immensely grateful but had not moved for so long that he was unable to do so even when the ropes were off him. Stiffness had set into old bones. Captain Smyth was set to massage blood back into his General's limbs. It was a painful process, and Farrar-Drumm cursed his efforts roundly, the more so on account of a certain lack of success.

'Damn useless! I've half a mind to send you back into the line, Smyth, and get an ADC I can rely upon.' Farrar-Drumm coughed and wheezed and beneath the rumbles from his chest began to plot what he should do when he could move again. He would be somewhat limited, he realised, without any weapons, but he might manage to seize a *jezail* or a knife ... a leap from the train onto the back of a Pathan, something of that nature perhaps, when the fight was at its thickest. On the other hand, perhaps not ... Farrar-Drumm felt a stab of anger at his own physical constrictions; it took two of his troopers to lift him into the damn saddle. It was growing darker and darker by the minute; Farrar-Drumm ordered his ADC to strike a match so that he could examine his timepiece.

'I'm sorry, sir, I have no matches.'

'No matches!' Farrar-Drumm said bitterly. Then the lightning came again, playing like fire about the train and the station, brilliant and fearsome. Farrar-Drumm, making an enormous effort, dragged out a turnip-shaped pocket watch and studied it.

A little after 7 p.m. That meant they had fourteen hours to go. Farrar-Drumm broke out into a cold sweat. He was no coward and he had faced shot and shell for most of his long life; but to be slaughtered on the seat of a railway carriage was far from a fitting end for a soldier.

He must do something about that.

After some cogitation, he called for Cunningham.

Eighteen

Through the darkness of the bridge, Colour-Sergeant MacTrease marched up to Ogilvie and slammed to the halt.

'B Company ready to march, sir.'

'Thank you, Colour. We have five minutes in hand yet.'

'Aye, sir.'

'Remember: complete silence. That's vital.'

'The Jocks have all been told, sir.'

Ogilvie nodded. At this stage, there was little more to say. His thoughts went ahead to Fiona, whose chances of survival through the night could not be assessed; and back again to his company, not all of whom were going to come out of the attack alive. His own mind and, he knew well, the minds of MacTrease and the men, were split: as a symbol, the gold bullion was important to the Raj and the Pax Britannica; but to risk the lives of the women and children was a fearsome responsibility upon not only the shoulders of the government in Calcutta but also upon those of the soldiers who were to execute the order. The safety or otherwise of these women and children would depend upon the achievement of total surprise in the first instance, and that was up to Ogilvie: the Pathans would be watching his own small force on the bridge as they would be watching Fettleworth's great division on the other side. Once Ogilvie's attack had gone in and he had won control over the signal box and its explosive potential, surprise would be ended and then it would be the speed of Fettleworth's attack that would count.

With the company standing to, Ogilvie checked the time by his watch, held in the palm of his hand in the light of a shaded guard lantern.

'One minute, Colour.'

'Aye, sir.'

Ogilvie listened to MacTrease's breathing; that and his own were the only sounds in the night's current stillness. The earth seemed to have settled down, and the warm wind had lessened. The skies were clear now of lightning, but there was cloud lying across the moon and the night was very dark though, as the clouds moved before the wind, there would be patches of moonlight.

'Now!'

MacTrease moved away, ghostlike, and got the men on the move. They went fast, muffling the slings of their rifles; all unnecessary items of equipment, such as waterbottles, had been left behind on the bridge to reduce the chance of noise. There was a little over half a mile to go for the signal box, standing out as a darker shadow in the night, with its Pathan guard so far unsuspecting; or so Ogilvie hoped. As the distance closed to some three hundred yards, he passed the word to halt and ordered the Scots to go down on their stomachs and remain still. Then he went forward alone for a close reconnaissance.

'The signal box, did you say earlier, Sar'nt-Major?'

'Aye, sir.'

'Not the stationmaster's office?'

'No, sir, the signal box. From there, sir, the Pathans would have the best view of anyone approaching.'

'From any direction?' Farrar-Drumm asked.

'Aye, sir. A fine all-round view.'

'Yes. That makes it more difficult, of course, but we shall do it, Sar'nt-Major.'

'We, sir?' Cunningham sounded startled. When, summoned some hours earlier, he had spoken to General Farrar-Drumm about the explosives and the fuse line, the General had not indicated any intention of accompanying him on his self-imposed mission to cut the suspected fuse trail and, if possible, seize control of the signal box and the firing mechanism. The news that Farrar-Drumm now intended to do so was dismaying. 'You're joining me, sir?'

'Yes, certainly. I would send no man out upon a task I was afraid to perform myself,' Farrar-Drumm said, shifting his stiffened limbs in his seat. 'It will be useful experience for my ADC as well.'

'With respect, sir,' Cunningham said, 'I believe one man alone would have a better chance.'

'Oh, nonsense, Sar'nt-Major, three will have a three times better chance. Suppose one of us should be killed? There will be two more to take his place.'

'One man alone, sir, would operate more anonymously. It's a job, sir, that must be done clandestinely. That is, sir, the cutting of the fuse line. The signal box—'

'Yes, yes, I take your point, Cunningham.' Farrar-Drumm nodded his head vigorously. 'They are two distinct and separate exercises – I agree. One man shall cut the fuse line – you, Sar'nt-Major, since it was your own idea. Captain Smyth and I shall attack the signal box.'

'Sir—'

'No argument, if you please, Sar'nt-Major,' Farrar-Drumm said loudly. 'My mind is made up. There is now the question of arms. We must rely upon being able to seize weapons from the Pathans, and since we shall have the advantage of surprise, I think we should be able to manage that. Captain Smyth will seize me a *jezail* and I shall give a good account of myself.' Farrar-Drumm looked out of the window as if reconnoitring his position. 'I believe a good moment has arrived, Sar'nt-Major,' he said. 'If we leave the train now, and descend by the door to the right of us ... the Pathans have gone from the immediate vicinity.' The General reached out a blueveined hand, a shaky one, and gestured out into the night. 'May God be on our side, Sar'nt-Major, and on the side of all those poor children.'

The First Division stood ready to advance, all preparations having been made under the cloak of darkness. Fettleworth was mounted in the van of his command, ready for anything. His sword was already drawn as he waited for Captain Ogilvie to show his guard lantern from the signal box in indication that the way was prepared for the main assault; Fettleworth had issued precise orders that the rifles were to remain silent for as long as possible, since their use might endanger the lives of the hostages: stray bullets could enter the coaches. The initial assault was to be carried out by the bayonet-blade alone and the killing was to be fast, the whole Pathan band being forced into engagement from the start so that they would have no time or opportunity to exact vengeance upon the hostages. Speed and an iron determination – those were the essentials. This could be left to the infantry; on either flank, the cavalry, who would ride to east and west as the general advance began, would press the Pathans inwards towards the bayonets or hack them down with their own sabres.

'Can't fail,' Fettleworth said as he waited in the saddle. 'There's only – what – some five hundred of the buggers. They'll be utterly overwhelmed in the first five minutes. What's happened to young Ogilvie, I wonder?' He peered anxiously ahead, watching for the guard lantern's light. 'I'd expected him before now, I must say, assuming he moved off on time, that is.'

Lakenham said, 'One should not expect things to go like clockwork, sir. Ogilvie may have met hindrances.'

'Yes, yes ... it'd be too bad if we fail at the last moment.' Fettleworth gnawed at the ends of his moustache. 'I can't risk advancing until that damn fuse line's rendered harmless. That's the crux of the whole thing. The very crux!'

Lakenham said nothing; Fettleworth was starting to fuss, and the less response the better. But a moment later there seemed a need for concern: rapid firing came from the darkness ahead, from somewhere in the train's vicinity.

Ogilvie, by approaching on his stomach through clinging mud until he was within some thirty yards of the signal box, had remained, he believed, unseen by the Pathans. Four of them were in the box itself, clearly to be seen in the light of a railway lantern. Each of them carried a bayoneted *jezail* and none of them seemed to be watching out particularly carefully, though every now and again a man would stare all round through the windows before leaning back with his *jezail* cradled in his arms. The train itself remained unlit as it had remained throughout, and there were few lanterns along the track. In the light from these few, Ogilvie could see the Pathans moving about or squatting by the line. All of them were well armed; but there was an overall air of restlessness, of tension ... Ogilvie believed this to be due to a fear that the earth tremors would return and grow rather than to any expectation of attack from the division encamped before them. If there had been any immediate expectation of this, the tribesmen would surely have been standing to with more alertness.

Ogilvie was about to turn and crawl back to his company and then lead them forward in silence when he saw a curious sight in the light coming from the windows of the signal box: a tall, thin, white-haired figure in British uniform, accompanied by another British-uniformed man, had set foot upon the ladder leading up the box itself. As Ogilvie recognised General Farrar-Drumm, whom he remembered well enough from a year or two before when the 114th had been attached to Southern Army, the two were evidently seen by the signal box's occupants. A *jezail* was lifted and the butt was smashed into a window; as the glass tinkled down, the Pathan opened fire and both figures vanished. As more shots came, Ogilvie moved fast. Now there was no more time for silence and surprise advances: at any moment, the fuse line would be lit and up would go the train. On his feet now, Ogilvie shouted for MacTrease to come forward at the double. Then, just as B Company pounded up, a cruel moon slid out from behind the clouds and lit the whole scene in brilliant silver.

That moon shone down upon General Fettleworth and the full array of the First Division. Bloody Francis looked petrified in the silvery light. 'The buggers'll see us now!' he said pathetically. 'I needed surprise, Lakenham!'

'Yes, sir. We should—'

Fettleworth flapped his hands. 'What shall

I do? There's no damn time—'

'You must advance, sir, without delay – at once!'

'That's all very well, but—'

'At once, sir!' The Chief of Staff stood in his stirrups, looming over Fettleworth and almost shouting at him in his urgency. 'If we don't move in, the Pathans will blow up the train – somehow, we have to prevent that! We can't wait for Ogilvie now.'

Fettleworth nodded. 'Yes, I suppose you're right, though I'd have thought they'd have done it already. Very well, Lakenham, sound the general advance, if you please.'

Lakenham raised his voice to the bugler. As the man sounded off, the cavalry trumpets took up the call and the mounted regiments at once galloped out to the flanks. At the same moment the infantry went forward at the double, with the shining bayonets held out before them as they charged the Pathan perimeter, where all seemed chaos, the *jezails* firing as it seemed in all directions at once. Men went down, throwing up their arms, screaming, but the advance of the division was unstoppable. In the signal box an independent fight was in progress, and Fettleworth, seeing it, cried out to Lakenham: 'Ogilvie's got there, thank God!'

'So it would appear, sir—'

'Detach some men to his assistance,

Lakenham.'

Lakenham looked around, then rode towards an infantry battalion and had breathless words with its colonel. A company was doubled out of the main advance to make for the signal box. A few moments later Lakenham found himself alongside the train; riding past the windows he was much relieved to find the coaches empty of Pathans and to see the excitement and relief on the faces of the hostages. Riding on as the British bayonets sliced and thrust into the Pathan bodies he approached the signal box. At the bottom of the steps he found two officers: one was Farrar-Drumm, who was cradling the head of the other upon his knees.

Lakenham pulled up his horse and saluted. 'Are you hurt, sir?' he asked.

'A flesh wound in my left arm, thank you. It's nothing. Poor Smyth has gone, however – my ADC, yer know.'

'I'm sorry, sir.'

'So am I, really. Stupid – but damn brave, doncher know. *Damn* brave. Where's that Sar'nt-Major, the Scottish one? Name's Cunningham.'

'I've no knowledge of him, sir—'

'Well, I suggest you find out at once,' Farrar-Drumm said briskly. 'He was going to cut the fuse line. I rather think he must have succeeded, or we'd all have gone to

Kingdom Come by now.'

Saluting again, Lakenham brought his horse round and rode away amid the stench of gunpowder, of blood, of many dead and gaping entrails. From the signal box, where the lantern had been overturned in the fighting, red fire flamed to bring a devilish light to the scene below. By now the train had been boarded by the infantry, and the hostages were being freed. Lakenham, coming upon a medical section, passed the word that General Farrar-Drumm was in need of attention. Then he came upon a pair of legs sticking out from under the central coach of the train, and once more he pulled up his horse. This time he dismounted; the legs were bare of trousers, and the stockings showed the tartan of the 114th Highlanders. Lakenham bent down: the sergeant-major was backing out now.

Lakenham said, 'Well met, Magnus Bareleg!'

Cunningham, looking startled, got to his feet and saluted. 'My name is Cunningham, sir—'

'I know, Mr Cunningham. My reference was to the Viking king who first wore the kilt and acquired the sobriquet thereby. Have you been cutting fuses, or what, Sar'nt-Major?'

'I've done more than that, sir. I've demolished the infernal machine itself, sir.'

'You have some knowledge of explosives, then, and of their handling?'

Cunningham said, 'Only a little, sir.'

'Then you're damn lucky to be alive, Sar'nt-Major – and so are we all, thanks-to you.'

'A very well conducted operation, I fancy,' Fettleworth said as he rode back into camp. He was very satisfied; those hostages who had survived the initial seizure of the train were safe to a man and though many were on the sick list their ills would be attended to by the leeches of Division. He had met a man named Wilberforce, a Civilian, who had showered praises, a rare thing for a Civilian to shower upon the military ... yes, matters had turned out well in the end. Not a Pathan had survived the slaughter. What the infantry hadn't got, the flank cavalry had. The First Division had suffered casualties, of course, but never a fight was won without sacrifice, and the men understood that. Fettleworth commanded very fine fellows, very brave fellows. As soon as he had the time he would assemble them and tell them so. Of course there yet remained the gold bullion, the stuff the whole affair had been about. It must be found; it must never be allowed to cross into Afghanistan. Bloody Francis refused to lose his soldiers' lives in vain. In the meantime, there was a mass of detail to be attended to. Reports must be prepared for despatch to Calcutta, and old Farrar-Drumm must be reunited with Southern Army as fast as possible, and God knew where Southern Army had got to ... and Lakenham had already had words about the sergeant-major of the 114th. Lakenham had suggested a recommendation for the Military Medal and it seemed a good idea...

During the next afternoon, when Fettleworth had taken his luncheon and a number of *chota pegs*, the advance of a Scots battalion was reported in the distance to the west. Within the next hour or so, the Royal Strathspey marched in, weary and mud-covered but marching smartly behind the pipes and drums. With them came a dirty figure in a once-white suit, borne along in a *doolie*. General Fettleworth, watching with his staff the arrival of the Scots, recognised his Political Officer, Blaise-Willoughby, his head almost invisible beneath many bandages. When Lord Dornoch halted his battalion, Blaise-Willoughby was carried forward to meet Bloody Francis.

'You look the worse for wear, Blaise-Willoughby,' Fettleworth said, and glared angrily at the monkey in its accustomed position. 'I see the damn monkey's survived again,' he added sourly.

Blaise-Willoughby was at the end of his

tether by now. He snapped, 'The damn monkey found the gold bullion as it so happens, General.'

'Oh, rubbish, and don't be blasted impertinent.' Bloody Francis' face had grown red; then he ticked over and his mouth sagged open. 'What? *What* did you say, Blaise-Willoughby?'

'Wolseley found the gold,' Blaise-Willoughby answered.

Bloody Francis was overcome; to have lost the gold would have been the blackest of marks upon his career and never mind the splendid way in which the operation against the Pathans holding the train had been conducted. 'My dear fellow,' he said solemnly, 'I do congratulate you! *Splendid* work – splendid! I am much pleased. Tell me about it, Blaise-Willoughby.' He put an arm round the Political Officer's shoulders in friendly fashion and yelled for his bearer. 'You'll take a *chota peg*, of course.'

Blaise-Willoughby, still aggrieved about the remark made against Wolseley, whose leg was still splinted, made his report in a tart voice, not the voice of the happy man who had found the stolen gold. He reported the circumstances of the discovery. After that he had, he said, been found by picquets from the Royal Strathspey and in an unconscious state had been screamed at by a colour-sergeant. When he had returned to consciousness and had felt fit enough, he had been placed in a *doolie* from which he had guided the Scots towards the cache of gold bullion.

'Yes, yes, my dear fellow,' Bloody Francis said, anxious to get to the nub. 'Where is the gold now?'

Blaise-Willoughby scowled and sighed. He said, 'I dare say you'll have noticed there have been earth tremors.'

'Yes, yes—'

'So there were up in the hills.' Blaise-Willoughby lifted clenched fists in the air and shook them, his face contorting. He was as upset as Fettleworth was going to be; there would be no accolades now, no handsome expressions of thanks from the Viceroy or Her Majesty or the Treasury. 'The bloody stuff's all gone ... a long way down, too. I suppose you could dig, but it would take a thousand or so years at a guess.'